DOWN
ROOT

Down Root

For information contact:
thistleboundbooks@yahoo.com

Cover Design by Angela Merkle
Template created by Derek Murphy

ISBN: 979-8-9866034-2-1

First Edition: December 2022
10 9 8 7 6 5 4 3 2 1

DOWN ROOT

Volume 1

Emily G. Watson

Thistlebound Books

EMILY G. WATSON

Table of Contents

EMILY G. WATSON

Author's Note

Down Root was originally supposed to be a serial (not cereal, a difference in spelling and definition that greatly confused me as a kid whenever they talked about serial killers). I imagined *Down Root* kind of like a tv show, where each volume was a season. So I apologize if the translation from that into a novella format feels a little disjointed.

This was also just a side project, something I was doing more for the fun. I fell in love with the characters and followed them "down the roots" so to speak, and the story really took on a life of its own. So here it is now, still something I intend to do more for the fun and enjoyment of it without taking too seriously.

So please enjoy, and don't take it too seriously yourself!

EMILY G. WATSON

Dedication

For all the crazy ones out there. Life is short. So when you find someone whose crazy matches your crazy, you got to stick together.

EMILY G. WATSON

1

A ROUGH
START

BY THE ANGLE OF sunlight filtering through the window, Ned immediately knew he had slept in, and he jerked his head up from the desk, papers and sketches and drawings he had been working on the night before scattering in all directions. Could he still make it? Challenge accepted. He practically dove into his jeans and pulled on his sweatshirt as he raced down the hallway, all while balancing a banana, a coffee mug, and his backpack.

He was fairly impressed with himself as he

slid into his seat just as the professor began his lecture. Not that his speed helped him understand anything the professor talked about. If it had been any other subject, he would have been fine. Give him a pile of rocks to analyze in geology lab or even something painful to read like *The Great Gatsby*, and he would plough right through. But business calculus at 9 am was pushing it. Derivatives and second derivatives were completely lost to him. He relaxed slightly as the class neared its end.

But too soon, for it was then that his worst fear came true.

"Mr. Parker," Professor Gates barked in his dry, nasally tone.

"Yes, sir?" Ned winced.

"What method should be used to find the second derivative of this equation?"

"Second what?"

"Mr. Mendoza, would you care to help Mr. Parker out here?"

Ned cringed in his seat as Spencer Mendoza smugly stood up and gave a detailed explanation of second derivatives and how to find them. Ned's girlfriend Mac rolled her eyes and sneaked an amused smile at him from across the room. For the rest of the class, Ned tried to hide behind his notebook, sinking lower and lower into his seat as he proceeded to become more and more confused about derivatives of any nature. When class finally ended, he breathed a long sigh.

"Do you feel how warm it is in here?" Mac spoke from behind him. "You must be feeling pretty burned."

"I believe 'roasted' would be the correct term." Chris Harper joined them.

"But then again, he did manage to show up on time today."

"That is an improvement. We are so proud of you, Ned."

"And you owe me ten bucks, Chris." Mac snapped her fingers and held out her palm.

"I think I should get some of that ten bucks. After all, you won the bet, but I did the legwork," Ned clicked his tongue, also holding out his hand. But behind them, he caught sight of Spencer leaving the classroom and his smile faded. *Show off.*

Mac followed his gaze. "How about I treat you to a slushie instead?" she said.

Awww, yis. Ned felt his mouth turn up at the corners again. "Ooo. Grape for me," he said, standing and shoving his notebook into his backpack.

"Dr. Pepper for me," Chris said. "Best food

3

creation *ever*."

"And we will explain derivatives to you while we're there," Mac promised.

Two hours and four slushies of sugary goodness later, Ned was finally able to grasp how to solve the problems. "Where would I be without y'all?"

"Completely lost," Mac said, and Ned was drowning once again. Only this time, in the eyes that he could never resist looking into.

She may have been petite, but Mackenzie's personality more than made up for her size. Dark hair, brown eyes, a round face, and a little turned up nose. Her eyes had a sparkle of mischief in them. She could be cool and collected one minute and dancing down the aisle the next. She could out-argue just about anyone their age, and she did it with a sharp tongue too. If anyone did try to get in a fight with her, they discovered it was like getting attacked by a deranged Pekingese. But around her friends, she was sweet, sassy, and a bit crazy. "Well, if you showed up to class once in a millennium, maybe you would understand things better."

"Touché," Ned sighed. "But if Rizzo's would stop offering dollar pizza after midnight, that would stop happening."

"Burned out on ramen noodles again, eh?"

"Life of a starving college student," Ned said. "Trying to save up money for a truck so that I can actually haul my own equipment when I go to a job. That, and my mind was going crazy with landscape designs last night. Had to get them down while I could. I'm hoping that I can convince a client in West U to go for one of them."

"Say, bro, you think you could use an extra hand with that this summer?" Chris asked. "Lookin' for some extra cash, and I am *not* going back to work for Waffle House."

"Sure! I'll hit you up when I get back from break. I'll be looking at getting customers' spring flowerbeds done, and then there will be a lot of projects heading into summer. Could definitely use some help." Ned scraped his chair back and planted a kiss on the top of Mac's head. "Thanks for the tutoring session and the slushies, but I've got to bail. I have Spanish, and then spring break can officially commence!"

"Did you call Nana yet?" Mac asked.

"Ooo, are y'all going to Nana's?" Chris's face brightened. "Bring me back some cookies will you?"

"Will do," Ned laughed.

It was a universally acknowledged truth that Nana White made the best cookies on the planet. Nana had been Ned's foster mother all throughout his teenage years until he moved away to go to college. But he came back to visit every chance he got. Nana and her granddaughter Robin were the closest thing to family that he had.

Robin and Ned had grown up as foster brother and sister. There were only two years between them, but Robin had always been shy and timid, so Ned tried to look out for her and protect her. Which had become harder to do after he left for college, and he worried about her constantly. He was relieved now that she was finally at the University of Houston as well. It was still hard to see her on a day-to-day basis because their schedules were completely opposite, but at least he was close by if she needed anything.

After Spanish class got out, he and Mac jumped on his motorcycle and headed north to Conroe. The live oaks and crepe myrtles of Houston gave way to the tall, stately pine trees of the Sam Houston National Forest. Nana lived on the outskirts of town in an old house with a sizeable yard that backed up to the national forest.

Nana herself was one of those amazing old

ladies that end up scaring you because they're so awesome. She was ancient looking, white-haired, and bespectacled, and always smelled like cinnamon. But don't ever let the old lady routine fool you. She also kept a shotgun under her bed and had been known to shoot skeet in her backyard. In other words, she was one of those comforting and fiercely protective Southern grandmas, who always seemed to know what to do and was always there for you.

She came out to meet them as they pulled into the gravel driveway. "Welcome home, Ned! Glad to see you brought Mackenzie with you. Although, you're doing her a disservice by letting her ride that motorcycle."

Ned winced as he drew back from giving her a kiss on the cheek.

"Ouch. You are just getting burned by everyone today," Mac laughed. "Hi, Nana."

"Good afternoon, dear. Now, I know you two just got here and are probably wanting to come inside, but I was wondering if Ned could come out back for a minute. Something's wrong with my geraniums, and I need you to take a look at them."

"Sure," Ned said. "I was going to try to get those tomato plants in today."

"Hey, Robin," Mac called.

Robin was walking towards them, wrapped in her red University of Houston hoodie, the wind blowing long dark strands of hair across her face. Usually when she spoke, her voice and eyes betrayed her timid nature, especially around people that she didn't know well. Around Mac and Ned though, she was at ease. "Hey, I heard the motorcycle and figured it was y'all."

"Robin, dear, would you show Ned the geraniums?" Nana asked. "I'm going to go get them something to drink. Sweet tea alright with everybody?"

"Yes, ma'am!" the three of them chorused together.

Nana chuckled and headed back up the driveway. "Alright, then. I guess it's unanimous."

The three college students headed round the house towards the back yard.

"So, how you doing, Robin?" Ned asked, putting an arm around her shoulders. "How are classes?"

"Oh, they're okay. My biology professor gave us an extra credit opportunity, so I may need you to help me with that."

"That I can do," Ned nodded. "Just don't ask about derivatives."

Robin smiled. "Rough day in class today, huh?"

"He got roasted," Mac volunteered.

"Well, he has all of spring break to cool down – "

"Oooo, that's not good," Ned bent over the geraniums planted along the gardening shed and pulled at a few leaves.

Robin hugged her arms to herself. "Yeah, Grandma noticed it just this morning when checking on the garden."

"It's some kind of rot." Ned dusted off his hands. "I've got some spray that might help take care of it. But if it didn't work, I'll have to pull them all."

"Aww, not Nana's geraniums!" Mac made a sad face.

"Honestly," Ned said, "would you really be sad to see the scrawny pathetic things go? I mean, they're pretty hideous."

"Hey! You may not like geraniums, but they're Nana's! She *adores* them!"

"Yes, and I can't for the life of me understand why. Don't tell her I said that."

The three of them spent the next hour planting tomato plants under Ned's directions. Nana kept them well supplied with sweet tea, and as they finished up, she brought them a plate of her legendary cookies. They sat on the back patio and stared out at the meandering flowerbeds and trees that stretched across the lengthy backyard while the national forest loomed in the background.

"It looks lovely, Ned," Nana said. "Did you find out what's wrong with my geraniums?"

"Yeah, it's some kind of rot. I'll work on it."

"I know you will," Nana smiled at him. "I'm sorry to take up your spring break with chores, but I'm getting old, and my body doesn't work as well as it used to. Well, has everyone had enough? I've got a dishwasher to run, and there's just room for these dishes."

"Here, let me help you," Mac offered. She and Nana collected the dishes and carried them inside.

"The garden really does look nice, Ned," Robin said. "You're the reason she always wins the Annual Garden Society Award, you know. How's the gardening business going, by the way?"

"Pretty well, actually! Most of the jobs are out in West University, so pretty expensive houses with beautiful yards. My mind keeps coming up with all these garden designs whenever I ride through there." Ned pulled a folder out of his backpack and showed her the drawings he had been working on the night before. "This is the one I'm wanting to try this summer in Nana's garden. But first, I'm going to need to replace the back fence." Ned held the paper up and tried to picture the sketched designs along the back fence in the distance.

"Morning glories and grapevines," Robin nodded approvingly. "It will look great over by the vitex."

"I also want to create a coastal prairie bed." Ned traced his finger on the paper.

"Pretty soon, you won't have any more lawn to mow."

"Just a lot of weeding."

"Hey, Ned!" Mac called from the back door. "Wanna run to the store? Nana wants some fresh bread for dinner tonight."

"Can do!" Ned called. "Let me wash up first."

"Can you guys get some popcorn too?" Robin asked as Ned and Mac prepared to leave. "Oh, and Nutella."

"Sure thing," Ned said as he pulled his gloves on.

"Wow, Robin, you should really find some

new friends to hang out with."

Ned sighed and turned to face the gate. Fergus Kennedy was walking up the driveway. As usual, his two younger brothers flanked him on either side. Today, he had a new face with him.

"Oh, boy," Ned muttered under his breath. "Here we go again."

"I mean really," Fergus said. "Still hanging out with these welfare cases? You could really do better than that."

The back of Ned's neck bristled in irritation. Fergus could call him names all he wanted – he'd been doing that since middle school anyways. But no one got to talk about Mac like that. "Hello, Fergus. Run out of neighborhood cats to terrorize?"

"No, actually, second derivatives."

Just how had Fergus heard about that? "Mmm, who's the new bodyguard?"

"Robin, I'd like you to meet my cousin, Roddy Kennedy."

Roddy stared at them from brooding brown eyes. Altogether, he was the spitting image of just another Kennedy. Tall, silky hair, sharp features. Those keen piercing eyes that immediately sized you up and analyzed all your weaknesses and strengths. Probably what made

Fergus Kennedy, Sr., such a successful lawyer.

The Kennedys lived close by, also next to the national forest, and they were the town's own darling bluebloods. Mr. Kennedy used his money and connections to maintain his privacy, setting up his family in a large house outside the city close to the forest. Unfortunately for him, the rest of his fortune went towards keeping his son out of trouble.

"We're having a party tonight," Fergus continued, taking a step forward. "We were wondering if you'd like to come."

Ned gritted his teeth as Robin took a step backward. Fergus was getting a little too close to Robin for comfort – hers *and* his.

"Thanks, but we've got plans for tonight," she said, eyes going wide with a deer-in-the-headlights look.

"Well, that's a shame, because I hear it's going to be wild." Fergus moved closer again, but this time, Ned stepped between them.

"Look, Fergus, she said no."

"I wasn't talking to you!" Fergus snapped. "I was talkin' to the girl."

"Her name is Robin."

"And what's yours, UFO Boy?" Fergus taunted.

Ned pursed his lips. Fergus was really a master of pushing all his buttons today.

"You see, Roddy?" Fergus pointed at Ned. "There's all sorts of stories about him. There's even some that think he was dropped here by UFOs."

Ned smiled. "Yeah, they sent me ahead to warn everyone."

"Warn everyone about what? An alien invasion?"

"No, actually, to warn everyone that Fergus Kennedy is a big fat – "

Fergus swung fast and without warning, knocking Ned to the ground.

"Fergus!" Robin screamed, jumping back. "Leave him alone!"

Without stopping, Fergus jumped on top of Ned, fists flying. Ned's legs were waiting for him, and he responded with a series of vicious kicks. Dust filled Ned's nostrils while gravel dug into his skin and Fergus's fists beat into his face and stomach. The two rolled around on the ground while Robin screamed at them to stop. Roddy stepped forward as if he were going to help his cousin. That's when Mac bashed him on the head with a motorcycle helmet, sending him stumbling to his knees.

"Don't you even think about it," she

warned coldly, standing over him with her motorcycle helmet poised to strike again. Her controlled anger and calm demeanor brought a chill to the air. The rest of the Kennedy clan hesitated. Roddy glared at her and put his hands up in surrender.

Then one of the younger Kennedy brothers screamed in terror.

"A gun!" he yipped. "She's got a gun."

2

PARTNERS IN CRIME

IT WAS INDEED NANA with shotgun at the ready, coming from the kitchen. "Fergus Kennedy, you get off of him this instant!"

Fergus didn't hear her, but Roddy reached over and grabbed his ankle, pulling him away from Ned.

"Enough," he said sternly. "Fergus, enough!"

Fergus caught sight of Nana and scrambled backwards. "Aww, come on, old lady."

"It seems to me you need a lesson in manners," she said. "Shall I give it to you?"

"No lesson needed," Roddy shook his head. Mac helped Ned to his feet.

"Good. Get off my driveway before I change my mind."

"Alright, alright, cool," Fergus shrugged, dusting off the front of his now-scratched-up leather jacket. "We're leaving. UFO Boy, you always get old ladies to fight your battles for you?"

"Knock it off," Roddy snapped, shoving his cousin down the driveway. "We're leaving."

Nana watched as Roddy herded his cousins down the street.

"Need some ice?" Mac grimaced, examining Ned's face.

"Nah, I'll be fine," Ned grunted. He ran his fingers through his hair and shook out bits of dust and gravel. *UFO Boy.* The name rang in his head like the pain in his various scrapes and bruises. "We'd better get going to the grocery store."

"Forget the store," Nana said. "You can go tomorrow."

Ned sighed. He hated feeling like he disappointed her. "I'm sorry, Nana. I didn't mean to start a fight."

"You didn't start it, Ned. Now, let's get you some ice."

You didn't say "no" to Nana, especially

when she was holding a gun. She marched them into the kitchen and ordered Ned to sit down at the table.

The kitchen was a cheery room, with terra cotta floor tiles and yellow wallpaper and white oak cupboards. In Ned's mind, it always conjured up images of Nana cooking, and Robin drawing a line down the middle of the brownie batter bowl to make sure they each got a fair share, and their annual gingerbread house making contest.

Robin helped Nana finish making dinner while Mac played nurse.

"I will say, that was pretty sweet when you bashed that guy over the head with your helmet," Robin said, trying to hide the shaking in her hands as she washed lettuce for a salad.

"See, using a helmet could save your life. Ow! Take it easy!" Ned pulled Mac's hand away from his head as she attacked his face with a hydrogen-peroxide-soaked rag.

"I don't know how much it's going to help against those Kennedy boys," Nana shook her head as she sliced tomatoes on her Texas-shaped cutting board. "They just keep getting worse every year."

"Do you think we could get a restraining order?" Mac joked, ignoring Ned's protests of pain and continuing to clean the scrapes on the side of his face.

"And I was really looking forward to spring break," Ned sighed. "Joy."

"What you need is some hot soup," Nana said. "Then you'll feel better."

"I'm sorry we don't have fresh bread to go with it."

"It's fine. I'll pull a loaf from the freezer. Don't worry about it."

Ned managed to successfully stop Mac's rag from coming any closer again. "I'd better go put the gardening tools away before it gets dark." He left through the kitchen door, heading back out into the garden. It was the only place he could clear his head, and he rounded the corner of the garage to have a few peaceful moments to himself. Let the words of the bully that had failed to mature since middle school blow away with the wind as the sun warmed his face.

After a few minutes of smelling the roses, he meandered back to put the tools in the garage. The space and scents of the garden were just what he needed. And he was ready to go inside to get spring break off to a better start.

Nana's hot homemade potato soup was a great way to celebrate the start of spring break.

Ned cheered up being surrounded by his girlfriend and family, especially when Nana produced cupcakes for dessert.

"This is a festive way to kick off spring break," Mac said, bouncing in her seat with excitement.

"Oh, believe me, the festivities are just getting started," Ned assured her around a mouthful of sprinkles and frosting. "Tomorrow, we break out The List."

Ned was up bright and early the next morning. No time to waste with The List waiting. Before heading down to breakfast, he stopped by Robin's room.

"Come in," she called when he knocked.

He burst open the door. "Good morning, Robin, are you ready to start this crazy week by breaking out The List?"

"You mean the annual Spring Break Bucket List?" Robin spun around in her desk chair to face him. "Of course. I will be down in a minute." She was smiling, but Ned caught the darker-than-usual circles under her eyes.

"Are you alright?" Ned frowned. "You don't

look like you slept well."

"Oh," Robin shrugged, looking down and picking at her fingernails, a nervous habit Ned recognized all too well. "Yeah, it's nothing."

But Ned wasn't fooled. "It's Fergus isn't it? That wasn't the first time he's been here, is it?"

"Well, obviously he's been here before," Robin said.

"You know what I mean."

Robin twisted a hairband around her fingers. "Yeah, he's been here a few times. But it's nothing."

"No, Robin, it's not nothing," Ned said. He sat down on the edge of the bed and took her hands firmly. "Do you even like the guy or want to go out with him?"

"No, he just always seems to pop up out of nowhere and try to flirt with me anywhere I go."

"What is he *stalking* you?" Ned's voice rose a couple of octaves, and so did the anger boiling in his chest.

Robin tried to shrug it off, which only made him more protective. "It's not that big a deal."

"*Yes*, Robin, *it is*. I saw the way he looked at you. Take it from me as another guy – he's up to no good. We need to do something about this."

"Ned, please don't get involved," Robin

pleaded. "I didn't know he would attack you like he did yesterday. It will be okay. Please, promise me you're not going to go confront him or get the police involved or anything."

Ned rolled his eyes.

"Ned, please. Just wait and let me think about this. And whatever you do: don't tell Nana."

Ned hesitated. "Okay." He stood up. "I guess I'll see you downstairs then."

"Thanks, Ned."

After Ned left Robin, he went straight to Mac's room.

"Hey, are you ready to start this List or what?" she asked as he came inside.

Ned closed the door behind him. "Mac, I need your help."

"What with?"

"It's to help Robin," Ned told her. "You remember the way Fergus was creeping on Robin yesterday? Apparently, that's not the first time Fergus has been here."

Mac frowned. "How bad is it?"

"I wouldn't be surprised if he was stalking her. Now, she's made me promise not to confront him, among other things, but given his reaction last night, I'm not so sure that would work anyways."

"Twit," Mac scowled, using their British chemistry professor's favorite insult. "What did you have in mind?"

"I've got an idea. Probably considered illegal, a bit rash, and foolish, but I'mma do it anyways."

"Ooooo, are you asking me to be your partner in crime?" Mac cocked an eyebrow.

"Yes, I guess that's what I'm asking."

"What's the job?"

"All I need you to do is help me distract Fergus for a few minutes."

"That's it?"

"That's all you get to know," Ned held up his hand. "If things go bad, I want you to have plausible deniability."

Mac sat back, regarding him for a moment. "Alright, I'm in, Mr. Big Words."

"Okay, then, we should probably head down before Robin and Nana get suspicious. We do have The List to discuss after all."

"When do we put this plan of yours into action?"

"I'll let you know."

Nana had made a scrumptious breakfast, complete with pancakes, hashbrowns, eggs, and bacon. The perfect way to start a morning. After eating and doing dishes for Nana, they broke out The List.

The List included all the activities they wanted to do over spring break. Sometimes they completed it, sometimes not. But it had become an annual challenge that they liked to try to do. This year's list already had a number of items on it, drawn from previous years and brainstorming over the last few weeks.

"So, let's break this down and prioritize," Mac began. She placed the list down on the wooden surface of the kitchen table in front of them. "Skydiving is a new one, I believe."

"Um, nooooooo." Robin leaned back in her chair with wide eyes.

"I believe Mac is the one who put it there in the first place," Ned laughed.

"We're all finally over eighteen," Mac pointed out, waving her hand.

"I am *not* going skydiving," Robin shook her head again. "I mean if you guys want to, you are more than welcome."

"What else is on the list?"

Mac sighed and looked down at the list to continue reading. "Laser tag, the rodeo, scavenger hunt, escape room, Six Flags, Lake Livingston, ren faire, picnic, barbecue, paintballing, bowling, mini golf, Lord of the Rings marathon. Cow tipping."

"That's not a real thing," Robin groaned.

"You never know til you've tried," Ned held up a hand.

Robin laughed and groaned at the same time. "Why do you two have to be so crazy?"

"Because when you find someone whose crazy matches your crazy, you got to stick together."

"So, what order do we want to put these it?" Mac asked.

"Excuse me." Ned scraped his chair back and stood up. "I gotta make a phone call. Be back in a minute."

He stepped through the door that led into the library and was only gone a few minutes, but when he returned, Robin was gone.

"Where'd she go?"

"She's getting a shopping list from Nana," Mac said. "What was with the phone call?"

"Well, actually, it was several phone calls. I needed someone who follows Fergus on Twitter. But I have ascertained where our mark is going to be later today. We just need to schedule events accordingly."

"I'm guessing we don't want Robin around when we execute the plan?"

"Preferably not," Ned said, sitting back down at the table.

"Okay, so, what activities can we do today, and then what excuse can we have later for going out by ourselves."

"Precisely. But I have somewhat of an idea for the latter."

"Which is?"

"Skydiving."

"Oooh, are you taking me skydiving?" Mac's eyes got their crazy gleam he loved so much.

"Robin doesn't want to come, making it the perfect excuse."

"You don't think we'll hurt her feelings?" Mac frowned.

"Meh, I've got an idea."

Just then, Robin returned, holding up a piece of notebook paper. "Okay, I've got the grocery list."

"Perfect. Let me go get my shoes upstairs," Mac said.

Ned waited until Mac had left the room, then cleared his throat. "Robin, I have a confession to make."

"Why? What did you do?" Robin asked in

alarm, her breathing coming a little quicker.

"I kind of planned a surprise for Mac. For today."

"Oh," Robin laughed a little in relief and her shoulders relaxed. "And what's wrong with that?"

"Well, it involves skydiving." Ned said. "I'm sorry. I already made reservations, and I had this big dinner planned. I probably should have told you sooner."

"No, no," Robin assured him, "don't worry about it. You two go on and have fun. I'm sure Mac will love it."

"You're sure you don't mind?"

"Ned, it's fine. I will catch up on some reading. That *Mageborn* book I've been meaning to get to won't read itself."

"I promise, we'll do something really big and fun tomorrow," Ned said, tucking a strand of hair behind her ear. "You pick something from the list, and we'll do it. Robin's Day."

"Sounds good," Robin smiled.

As Mac came thundering back down the stairs, Ned gave her a thumbs up behind Robin's back.

Mac nodded in acknowledgment. "We ready to go to the store?"

"I guess we'll borrow Nana's truck," Ned

said as he picked the keys off the rack by the back door. "I don't think she would approve if we all tried to cram onto my bike."

"Yeah, that would not go over well," Robin grimaced as she imagined the the scene that would cause.

"There would be blood," Mac said dramatically. "Let's go then!"

"The mark has arrived." Mac lifted her sunglasses slightly so that she could peer under them.

"Listen to you, using fancy words and all," Ned said.

Across the street from them, Fergus and company were just exiting the steakhouse on the far side of the open square. Ned and Mac shifted slightly so that they were hidden by some shrubbery. The Woodlands Mall was busier than usual, and it wasn't hard to get lost in the crowd of people streaming up and down the streets and sidewalks, in and out of restaurants, Barnes & Noble, and stores with ridiculously over-priced clothing.

"So, what's the plan?"

"I'm going to go in. I may bump into him.

What I need you to do is jump in before he attacks me again. We'll act all conciliatory."

"Conciliatory," Mac echoed. "Look at you, using big words."

"Shut up. Your job is to distract him from the fact that I bumped into him. You know. Don't be yourself. Be sweet, calming, apologetic – ouch!" Ned winced as Mac pinched him.

"I get the idea," she rolled her eyes and shoved her sunglasses back into place. "Go on."

Ned maneuvered his way down the street and across and back up so that Fergus wouldn't see him approaching. Then he sneaked up behind Fergus and bumped into him.

"Hey, watch it," Fergus started. "*You* again." He narrowed his eyes and doubled his fists, and the other Kennedys closed in around Ned.

"Hey, I am so sorry," Ned backed up. "You know, I must have tripped on something." He backed straight into Roddy. "Listen, I just wanted to talk about what happened yesterday. Hope there are no hard feelings."

"Watch it," Fergus growled. "The old lady ain't here to protect you this time."

"Well, what do you know?" a voice interrupted from behind him. Mac smiled sweetly beneath her sunglasses. "Are y'all enjoying spring break?"

"What are you doing here?" Fergus glared.

"I'm here with Ned. There's no law against that." Mac linked her arm through Ned's. "Look, about yesterday, we are just so sorry. If there's any way we can make it up to you, please do let us know. But you know, you really did come off better than Ned. Not a scratch on that face! I guess we know who the better fighter is."

"Thanks, dear," Ned muttered under his breath.

It worked on Fergus though. "Yeah, I'm pretty good with my fists. Don't let your boyfriend here forget it."

"Oh, trust me, she won't," Ned said.

"Well, y'all enjoy your spring break," Mac said. "We need to be going."

They broke out from the circle of Kennedys and strolled down the sidewalk, arm in arm, smiling and looking as innocent as possible.

"Not too fast," Ned said between his teeth. "They'll get suspicious."

They turned a corner and ducked behind a potted plant. From there, they looked back to watch the Kennedys.

"It doesn't look like they're coming after us," Ned said in relief. "Doesn't look like they're suspicious either. Just annoyed."

"He'll be even more annoyed when he discovers he's missing this," Mac said, holding up Fergus's wallet.

Ned snatched it from her. "Hey, where'd you get that? And now you've put your fingerprints all over it." He wiped the outside of the wallet down with his shirt.

"From your back pocket," Mac rolled her eyes. "You really expected me to believe that that little performance was supposed to send him a message? It was obvious with that little bump that this is what you were after."

"You are sneaky aren't you," Ned said, shaking his head ruefully. He opened the wallet to find Fergus' face glaring back up at him. "He should know better than to keep so much cash in here. Look at his driver's license. You think he even knows how to give a real smile?"

"So, we just picked the pocket of the kid of one of the richest families in the greater Houston area," Mac said. "What do we do now?"

3

Monsters in the Dark

"I IMAGINE WE'RE IN enough trouble as it is," Ned said. "We should probably make the best of it. How about a night out on the town? Sky's the limit, up to five hundred dollars."

"Why five hundred?"

"Because anything over that and it's no longer a Class B misdemeanor."

"Gotcha. Keep it simple."

"We're only looking to annoy and inconvenience."

"Cool. But I'm pickin' the restaurant," Mac

said.

"Just so we're clear," Ned stopped her sharply, "if anyone asks, you didn't know. You had nothing to do with this."

Mac started to say something snarky but stopped when she turned and saw his serious expression. "Okay, I understand."

"Good."

"You're going to need me to bail you out."

Ned chuckled. "Exactly."

They certainly did have fun while it lasted. First, Ned insisted on treating Mac. Using the cash, he bought her some earrings, a necklace, and flowers. Then Mac insisted they buy something for Ned, so they bought him a nice leather jacket.

"That will look good when you ride your bike," Mac said

By then it was getting late, so they decided to finish with dinner and ice cream. All in all, as they sat on the curb in front of Ben & Jerry's licking mounds of delicious ice cream off of crunchy waffle cones, they decided it was worth it.

Until shortly after they had pulled up into the driveway at Nana's. As they climbed off the bike, Fergus' sports car appeared out of nowhere and screeched to a halt at the end of the driveway, spraying gravel in all directions.

"Mac, get inside!" Ned ordered.

"Parker!" Fergus roared, pounding up the driveway.

Ned did his best to keep the motorcycle between them. But Fergus came leaping over it, and they both ended up in the gravel again. Dust, gravel, and fists flew in the air. Ned pounded at Fergus' chest and stomach as Fergus ground Ned's head into the ground.

"Get off him," Mac yelled, delivering several well-aimed kicks and bashing away with her helmet.

But Fergus was in too much of a fury. Then everyone else arrived at once. Nana and Robin came running out of the house. A police car pulled up, sirens blasting and lights flashing. Two police officers and Mr. Fergus Kennedy, Sr., stepped out.

"Fergus!" Mr. Kennedy shouted.

The police were quick to pull Fergus and Ned apart.

"What is going on here?" Nana demanded. "Officers, this is the second time this week this boy has attacked my son!"

"Ma'am," one of the officers addressed her, "I'm Officer Briggs. This is Officer Dawson. I guess this is a more complicated situation than we thought. Are you Ned Parker?" he directed the question at Ned.

"Uh, yes, sir," Ned panted, still trying to catch his breath.

"There!" Fergus shrilled, holding something high above his head for all to see. "I told you he had it!"

Officer Briggs took the wallet from Fergus' hand and flipped it open. "You sure you weren't posing for a mug shot?" he asked, examining Fergus' driver's license. Then he turned his attention to Ned. "Son, this young man believes you to have stolen his wallet."

"That's ridiculous," Robin protested. "Ned..." She stopped and dropped her face into her palm.

"He claims to have found it on his person. Care to explain this, son?"

"Uh, nope. Not really."

"Well then, we're going to have to take it back to the precinct and dust it for prints. And we're going to go ahead and take you in as well."

"Hands against the car," Officer Dawson instructed.

Ned did as he was told and braced himself as the officer produced a set of handcuffs.

"I knew it was you," Fergus yelled as his father and Officer Briggs held him back. "You dirty thief!"

"Well, if you weren't stalking Robin, maybe we wouldn't have a problem," Ned said. "Or at least, as big of one."

"I assume, Mr. Kennedy, that once we run the prints, you'll be pressing charges?" Dawson asked.

"Certainly," Mr. Kennedy said, fixing Ned with a cool stare as he straightened his perfectly tailored gray bespoke suit.

"Just a minute," Nana interrupted them all, fixing Ned with a stare of her own, but this one held a question.

Ned understood the question and gave a nod in the affirmative.

Nana narrowed her eyes and cleared her throat. "Officer, while we're all pressing charges here, I'd like to press some of my own against this ill-behaved and conceited youth, Fergus Kennedy."

"Charge him with what?" the father of the ill-behaved youth demanded.

"Oh, I don't know. Trespassing. Two charges of assault. And how about a restraining order to keep him from stalking my granddaughter?"

"You can't be serious?" Mr. Kennedy, Sr., winced. Even he knew better than to pick a fight with Nana.

"Oh ho ho!" Nana's voice held a dangerous dare.

The two officers looked at each other.

"Very well," Briggs sighed. "Son, put your hands behind your back," he instructed Fergus.

"Aww, come on," Fergus yelled as the handcuffs closed around his wrists. "Dad!"

"Just be quiet," Mr. Kennedy glared at him. "You're in enough trouble without me having to come and bail you out every time."

"Should we send for another car?" Dawson asked.

"It's late, and I don't need the aggravation. So long as they promise not to kill each other, I think we'll be fine."

"I'm not the one who attacked first," Ned said.

"Son, if you so much as touch him, I will not hesitate to use my taser. I don't care how rich and powerful you think you are. Got that?" Briggs glared at Fergus.

At first, Fergus looked too taken aback to answer. Then as the officers proceeded to put him and Ned into the back of their car, he started loudly protesting again, yelling for his father to do something. He continued to whine as they cruised through the neighborhood. Occasionally, he would mutter threats against both Ned and the officers. Threats to get Ned back, and did they know his father was one of the most important lawyers in the state? He would have the officers' jobs!

While Briggs and Dawson continued to get more irritated and told Fergus to shut up and they didn't care how rich his dad was, Ned did his best to tune them out and ignore them. He looked through the barred window out at the forest flashing by. As nervous as he should have been, he couldn't help feeling a calm resignation. He had made a decision, had only been trying to help Robin, to get back at Fergus and scare him off, and he was going to stick by it. Looking out over the forest brought him calm, and the trees gave him a sense of serenity. Then he frowned and craned his neck forward to try to see better. What was that? He caught something moving out of the corner of his eye.

"Stop the car!" he shouted.

Officer Briggs slammed on the brakes as an enormous log fell across the road and smashed onto the front of the car. All of them were thrown forward by the impact, airbags slamming the officers back into their seats; it took a few moments for them to recover.

"Wow, that was close," Briggs groaned. "Everybody alright?"

"Yep," Dawson replied, dabbing at some blood on his forehead.

"Nope," Fergus moaned from the back.

"Sharp eyes, son," Briggs said to Ned. "Second later and we'd all be dead."

Fergus winced. "I think my nose is bleeding." He stopped. "Do you have any idea how annoying it is to have a nosebleed and not be able to reach it?"

"Enough, kid," Dawson growled.

"Did anybody else hear that?" Ned asked.

"Shhh," Briggs hissed.

A large heavy thump pounded through the air and shook the car ever so slightly.

"Don't go anywhere," Dawson said as he took of his seatbelt and drew his gun. "We'll be back."

Not like we can anyways. Ned watched the two officers circle to the front of the car.

Briggs continued to look about, scanning the road and the trees and everything else, while Dawson inspected the damage to the hood of the car.

"No way we're driving out of here. Better

call for backup," he told his partner.

There was another large thump, this time even closer, and then a large chunk of a tree came flying out of the forest. Dawson dove to the ground to avoid being hit. Briggs crouched down in front of the car and fired two shots in the direction it had come from.

A deep yell sounded from the forest, and then something came charging out of the woods. The two officers dashed back and retreated. Ned blinked hard. Was he seeing things?

"What was that?" Fergus gurgled in shock

"I don't think that was human," Ned said slowly. His voice shook slightly, but he was surprised at his own apparent calm.

He turned and ducked just in time as something broke through the window beside him and tried to grab him.

"Jack!" a gravelly, deep voice growled.

Another gunshot rang through the air, and the gnarly, giant, brownish-green hand jerked back through the window. Dawson's next shot hit the whatever-it-was in the shoulder. Whatever-it-was decided the officers were a more immediate problem than Ned. Outside the car, there was yelling and the sounds of fighting.

Ned squirmed and wriggled, feeling for the

button to undo his seatbelt. Hot sticky blood ran down his arms from the glass, and he was aware of pain, screaming to be registered in his brain. But adrenaline surged through his body and blocked it out. In a similar way, the fact that what he had just seen was not possible, was not human, screamed to be recognized, but his body and mind were in survival mode. The focus he needed to function at this moment blocked everything out and kept him going. His hands were cuffed behind him, but after much squirming and writhing like a contortionist, he finally managed to get his hands in front of him.

Okay, now what? He glanced over at Fergus. *Perfect!* He reached over and grabbed Fergus' fraternity pin off his jacket.

"Ow, hey!" Fergus yelled.

Ned ignored him and used the pin to pick the lock on the handcuffs. *Finally!* The cuffs came off one hand and dangled from the other like an oversized bracelet. He climbed through the window that had been smashed to pieces and slithered to the ground, ducking down behind the trunk of the car.

He dared a peek round the car's bumper. Dawson was pinned to the ground by what looked like a giant, gnarly... creature. It resembled and stood like a human, but taller, wider, stronger, and strangely proportioned. Briggs was running in zigzags around another monster, trying to get back to his gun which lay several feet away on the pavement.

Ned took a few deep quick breaths and then jumped out from behind the car.

"Hey, you!" he shouted waving his arms. "Over here! Come and get me!"

Unfortunately, his plan worked. The monster holding Dawson down on the ground looked up and immediately released his quarry. Ned caught a glint of white tusks as it came charging after him. He ducked back around the car and into the woods. Using trees and bushes as cover, he zigzagged, trying to keep ahead of the monster. Behind him, he could hear shots being fired. Hopefully, that took care of one of the monsters.

He turned to double back to the road, back towards the officers with the guns so that they could actually kill the thing, but he found that the monster was closer than he had thought.

"Jack!" it roared.

"My name is Ned," he retorted. He darted to one side, but the monster was quick to follow his movements.

"Jack be nimble, Jack be quick!" the gravelly

voice sang as Ned weaved from side to side, trying to get past.

He made a final desperate lunge, barely managing to scrape by. As he neared the road, he tripped over a root and fell. The monster caught up to him, catching him by the foot and swinging him up against a tree. Ned's head exploded with pain, and his vision swam. Then the monster pinned him by his chest against the tree.

"Where is it?" the gravelly voice asked.

"Where's what?" Ned tried to say, but the air was being crushed out of him.

More shots were fired as one of the officers (Ned couldn't tell which one at this point) emptied the rest of his magazine at the creature. Ned dropped to the ground. Maybe it had something to do with his head splitting and his blurry vision, but as he looked over at the body of the monster beside him on the ground, it looked as though the monster was turning into mud. It was all too confusing, and he closed his eyes.

4

LEGEND HAS IT

WHEN NED OPENED HIS eyes, he was standing outside a pavilion in the middle of a forest. A few of his friends were there, as well as a great many other people he didn't know. But for some reason, everyone seemed to know him. Nana was there. Robin was wearing a deep red dress, while Mac was dressed all in white with a garland of flowers in her hair. They were all dancing in circles around a maypole. Mac tilted her head back, and her laugh drifted over him like a bell. It was calming and soothing, and all at once he was fighting to keep his eyelids from drooping.

They were no longer in the forest but in a meadow. Snow swirled all around them. As Ned grew colder, Mac was slowly fading from his vision. A numbing chill crept through him, and sleepiness washed over him. Mac was leaning over him, telling him it was time to wake up.

No, it really was time to wake up.

Ned opened his eyes and was rewarded with an immediate flash of pain as the light hit his eyes. He snapped them closed again.

"Ned, wake up," Mac said severely.

"I'm awake," he managed to say. Breathing was difficult and took a ridiculous amount of energy.

"How are you feeling?" Robin's voice asked in a tremulous tone.

"Mmm." Ned took stock of himself. "There's a nail in my head and an elephant on my chest."

"Not surprising after that gang attacked y'all in the police car," Mac said. "Here, I've got a cold pack for your head. That should help a little."

"Thanks. Would someone mind turning down the lights and maybe closing the blinds?" Ned asked. "The light hurts."

"Oh, sure." He heard Robin's light footsteps

cross the room. "Is that better?"

Ned cracked an eye open, then the other. "Oh, much better. Thanks, Robin."

He could now see that they were in a hospital room. Mac and Robin were sitting on either side of his bed. Outside the door, he caught a glimpse of Nana and Fergus Kennedy, Sr., talking in hushed and urgent tones.

"What's going on?"

"I don't know," Mac said. "But seeing as you helped save Fergus' and those deputies' lives, I should think they'd be grateful."

"A gang?" That didn't sound quite right. Ned tried to remember.

"That's what the deputies said," Robin said. "Must have been some gang, too! They looked terrified."

"I'm sure they did," Ned said. His mind flashed back to the attack on the police car. Those gnarly monsters would have scared anyone. Or had he imagined the whole thing? Apparently, the deputies were going with a different story.

"Welcome back to the land of the living," Nana interrupted his thoughts. She came up to his bedside and patted his foot through the covers.

"Hi, Nana." Ned gave a sore smile.

"How are you feeling?"

"I've definitely felt better," Ned said. "I'd say I'm in a hurry to get out of here, but then again… I guess jail is waiting when I get out."

"I'm afraid there's not going to be any jail," Nana said. "Much as you probably deserve a few days in the tank."

Ned winced. "Yeah, probably."

"Both sides have agreed to drop the charges for now, especially seeing as you helped save Fergus' life."

"How on earth did you manage that?" Robin asked.

"Mr. Kennedy and I have come to… an agreement," Nana said. She studied Ned and Robin for a moment. "I'm going to go fetch a nurse. We'll see what we can do about getting you home."

"That would be wonderful," Ned said. As he struggled to piece together what had happened, he just wanted to be home and in a safe place.

After they had spoken with the doctor, he finally agreed that Ned could go home. So long as he stayed in bed or on the sofa for a few days. It wasn't exactly how Ned had planned on spending spring break, but it was better than jail.

Before they left the hospital, Briggs and Dawson came to see him. Both of them looked a little worse for wear, sporting Band-Aids and a few bruises.

"Glad to see you're going to be okay," Dawson said with a nervous smile. "Wanted to thank you for saving my life."

Ned nodded back in acknowledgment, regretting the instant headache it gave him. "So, it was a gang, was it?"

Dawson went red and swallowed, shuffling his feet.

Briggs sighed. "Look, kid," he said, "I don't know what we saw, but you go telling everyone you saw giant monsters attack you (which disappeared and turned into mud as soon as they were killed), and you're going to have much bigger problems than worrying about whether you stole some rich kid's wallet. So the only way this works is if we all stick to the same story."

"I totally agree, sir," Ned said.

"Good then," Briggs relaxed a little. "I just wanted to make sure we were on the same page. You did good out there, kid."

Ned was more than a little relieved to be back at Nana's house as he made his way through the entryway towards the kitchen and living room. He was able to walk without help, but it was slow going, and he was definitely going to be sore for a while.

"Actually, we're going into the library," Nana stopped him. "Come on, you can sit on the big sofa. Robin's making tea."

Ned turned to the glass paned double doors on his left that led into the library. Dark cherry wood bookshelves reflected the light from the flames flickering in the fireplace. The shelves lined the walls, surrounding them with books of all shapes and sizes: crisp new volumes, expensive leatherbound, dusty old tomes that hadn't been opened for decades. The diamond-paned windows looked out onto the front yard and the street over the tops of the azaleas Ned had planted in the front flowerbeds. On the opposite side of the room, a swinging door led to the kitchen. A bronze statue of a cowboy sat nestled on one of the coffee tables in the corner, while a saber and rifle, both used by Nana's father during WW1, were slung over the fireplace. Ned had never been one much for reading, but he had always loved hanging out in there, doing homework or puzzles with Robin and Nana, or playing games with friends.

"Why are we in here?" Ned settled into the big comfy sofa that let you sink just the right amount.

Robin placed a tea tray on the big coffee table in the middle of the room and handed Ned an ice pack. Then she and Mac sat down on either side of him.

"As per my agreement with Mr. Kennedy," Nana leaned back in her armchair, "I have something very important that I need to tell you – you and Robin. Mackenzie, I'm sorry, but I'm not so sure you should be here."

"Something tells me I'd rather she were," An uncomfortable feeling settled in Ned's stomach.

"Well, I guess she'd find out anyways." Nana studied him carefully for a minute. "Ned, what do you remember about the night they found you?"

Of all the questions that Nana could have asked, Ned was not expecting that one.

He had been in the hospital for a week. He had been found in the woods after having been struck by lightning, but no one could explain who he was or how he got there. And Ned couldn't tell them either. He couldn't remember anything. Drifting in and out of consciousness, he was unable to move his body that was covered in burns. The paralysis was temporary, but the lightning left its scars.

Until Nana arrived. She had shown up at the hospital looking for him, her foster son. He liked to play in the woods, she said. He must have gone wandering before the storm started and gotten lost. She had been looking all over for him.

Nana had taken him home, raising him alongside her granddaughter Robin. She had done her best to take care of him and help him remember, but there was nothing there to remember. It was gone. That was eight years ago.

So what did all of this have to do with that night?

"Not much," Ned said after a moment. Of course, Nana already knew he didn't remember anything. But if she was asking about it now, it had to be important. "It's all kind of hazy. The main thing I remember is waking up in the hospital and not being able to move."

"And before all that?"

"You know I don't remember anything before that. I couldn't even remember my name until you told it to me."

"Yes, about that. Your name isn't really Ned."

"It's not?" Mac wrinkled her eyebrows in confusion.

"What else would it be?" Ned asked. Nana was only making his headache worse. "And what does this have to do with the Kennedys and last night?"

"Alright, this is going to be a long and complicated story, so please don't interrupt me, no matter how strange it gets."

"Okay," Ned agreed somewhat hesitantly.

"Now, once upon a time, there was a boy whose name was Jack," Nana began. "He was always getting into some kind of trouble, that one. He and his mother lived on a farm near the town where I grew up, albeit many generations before. They were just struggling to get by. So one day, his mother sent him to town to sell their only cow. They just could not afford to keep her any longer, and they were going to use the money to buy a new plough.

"Well, no one in town wanted the cow unfortunately, but as he was heading home, Jack ran into a strange man who offered to buy it from him. In return, he would give something unbelievably precious and rare: three magic beans."

"Jack and the Beanstalk?" Mac queried with a doubtful expression.

"I said don't interrupt me," Nana scowled. "Now, I suppose you all think you know what happened next. Jack got into a heap of trouble with his mother. But she said to go ahead and plant the beans: they might as well get something out of the deal. But the beans did indeed prove to be magical. They sprouted in the middle of the night and grew into two large thick stalks. Kept half the countryside up. Created a miniature earthquake. Early the next morning, Jack climbed the beanstalk to see how high it went. And he did, as the stories say, discover a land of giants. You know what happened. He stole from one of them. It chased him down one of the beanstalks; he cut it down and killed the giant.

"Well, the giants were none too happy about that and came down the other stalk demanding Jack's head, and rightly so. So the king had Jack arrested, and Jack had his left hand cut off. He was also sentenced to slavery in the stone quarries."

"That's a bit harsh," Ned said.

"Yes, they actually punished thieves in those days," Nana said dryly.

Ned sank lower into the sofa as his ears

burned.

"After that, the giants were relatively peaceful," Nana continued, "and trade with the giants became very profitable for many people in the land. There wasn't much trouble to speak of – until Thumbling."

"I'm lost," Ned said.

"Tom Thumb." Mac pinched him. "Do keep up."

Ned glanced over. She was thoroughly enjoying this.

"There are many different versions of the Thumbling story, and only one comes close to what really happened. Thumbling was indeed born the size of a thumb, out of the wish of an old couple who just wanted a child. But one day out in the fields, he met with a giant. The giant took him and raised him, feeding him giants' food and giants' drink. Thumbling grew up to be as tall as any giant, and stronger than any giant too. His giant father was proud of his strength, but in his heart, Thumbling was nothing more than a spoiled bully, who had been taught that physical strength would get him anything he wanted.

"He returned home to his human parents, but they didn't even recognize him at first. It became obvious that they couldn't feed him, and besides that, they were afraid of him. So Thumbling went on his way, taking whatever he wanted by brute force. And it was never enough, until finally, he decided that he would have the kingdom. He went on a rampage, destroying everything in his path, with the help of a horde of ogres. He made it to the castle, where he declared himself king. Meanwhile, many of the people had fled to the beanstalk."

"But wouldn't that just take them to giant land?" Mac asked. "I mean, would the other giants have helped them or no?"

"If you climbed *up* the beanstalk, you would end up in giant land, yes. And well, many of the giants were friends with Thumbling. But you could also climb *down* the beanstalk. At the end of its roots deep in the earth lay, well, here. And a giant was too big to follow.

"One of these people running away to this world was a young boy, who also incidentally was named Jack. This Jack helped to make sure that as many people as possible made it safely down, or up, into this world. But he knew that even if Thumbling couldn't follow them, the ogres would. So Jack chopped the beanstalk down to close the portal. Only, it was struck by lightning just as he hit it with the axe."

"I can relate to that," Ned shuddered.

"Ned," Nana's voice became quiet, "when he did recover and woke up in the hospital, he couldn't remember anything. And no one could know who he was. So I decided to call you Ned."

Ned stared at her for a moment, trying to hold back, but the laugh finally escaped him as he lowered the cold pack from his head. Pain tore through his chest, reminding him that bruised ribs and cartilage still existed.

5

THE DOLDROMS OF RESEARCH

"NED, THAT'S... SO COOL!" Mac breathed, eyes a twinkle.

"You do know you're beginning to sound as if you believe her," Ned muttered, trying to recover from the spasms of pain in his chest.

"It's a good story."

"So, you're trying to say that Ned is Jack," Robin spoke slowly with heavy sighs in between each word. "The second Jack."

EMILY G. WATSON

"Yes," Nana nodded.

"Nana, I don't mean any disrespect," Ned said, grunting a little at the pain in his chest. "But that's... ridiculous..."

"Oh, so those ogres who attacked you last night – that's ridiculous too?" Nana raised an eyebrow.

Ned felt his face going red as he opened and closed his mouth, but he couldn't find a reply. He couldn't meet her eyes, because he knew the monsters hadn't been all in his head. They had been real after all. "It just doesn't – "

While he was looking down at his lap, Nana dropped something into it. It was one of the dusty, old, leather-bound volumes from the bookshelves. On the page that she had opened to was a hand-drawn picture of several men being attacked by a monster, just like the ones that had attacked last night.

"Wait, so you weren't attacked by a gang?" Robin asked.

"I had a hunch it was ogres, and I can see I was right," Nana said. "You should consider yourself lucky. Most people get a lot worse when they're attacked by ogres."

Ned and Mac looked at each other, then stared straight ahead at the far wall as they tried to process what Nana had just said.

"Wait, so you said you're from there, the place on the other end of the beanstalk," Robin frowned. "Where did I come from then?"

"You were born 'Up Root' as they call it," Nana said. "Your parents died when you were only a toddler, so I moved you here to be with me. It is just like I have always told you about your parents. Only, you don't remember Up Root because you were just far too young. And obviously, with the beanstalk cut down, there was no way to take you there when you were older."

"What about my parents?" Ned asked, nervous with hope and fear all at the same time. "Do I have any family? Were they..."

Nana's face fell, and she bit her lip. "I'm sorry, Ned, I don't know. You only had your mother. I looked for her, but I wasn't able to find her. Some said she came through the beanstalk with you, but then she disappeared. We never saw her again."

Ned could only nod, the sudden burst of hope and curiosity squashed down. He leaned forward, elbows on his knees, swallowing hard as his eyes burned. This – this hurt more than anything else. To know he did have a mom, a family, out there, only to have lost them again. Mac put a gentle hand on his shoulder.

After a few deep breaths, he forced himself back to the more immediate problems. As he studied Nana, he knew there were many pieces of the story she wasn't saying. Things that just didn't add up. Like how did Nana know about Ned? And how had she come to be his 'foster mother'?

Much as he wanted answers, he knew that there was more urgent business to deal with right now. Like the ogre attack. They had been after him specifically. What were they after? Was that why Nana had felt the need to change his name and hide him?

Something else was bothering him, and he finally found his voice. "So, what deal did you make with Mr. Kennedy? What does he have to do with any of this?"

"Oh, the Kennedys are old Up Root blood. They came through the beanstalk long before Thumbling's invasion, generations ago. Mr. Kennedy reached the same conclusions about the attack the other night as I did."

"He knows who I am?" Ned raised his eyebrows.

"Only other person besides me."

Ned wasn't quite sure how he felt about that. "Fergus doesn't know about all this, does he?"

"I'm not sure how much he knows," Nana said. "Fergus was born and raised here. I'm not sure how much he knows about Up Root or you."

"What exactly was the bargain?"

"I tell you about everything. And keep you safe. If those ogres are coming back, they'll be coming back for you."

"Why me?"

"Because of the axe."

"What axe?"

"To cut the beanstalk, you used a magical axe, an enchanted axe that could cut through anything," Nana explained. "One of the greatest legendary weapons of Up Root. And Thumbling wants it. So he's after you because he thinks you have it."

"Well, the last time I checked, I didn't have a magical axe," Ned said. "Unless there's something about the one out in the shed you want to tell me."

Nana gave a small smile at his attempt at a joke. "No, you don't. The axe also disappeared after the lightning strike. No one knows what happened to it."

"What do we do now?" Robin asked. Her voice had that tremulous tone it always got when she was terrified of something. "Are they going to come back?"

"Doubtless," her grandmother replied. "And we need to find that axe before they do."

"Where do we start?" Mac asked.

"A lot of people have already combed the national forest, looking for it near where the beanstalk used to be. They never found it. I suggest we turn to another form of research."

"Which is?" Ned asked.

"Books," Mac guessed. "Newspapers, the web. There have to be stories about it. If we can trace where the most recent stories came from, then maybe we can find out where the axe was last seen."

"You mean we have to read?" Ned gave her a pained look.

Mac pinched him again. "You are unbelievable."

"Not tonight, anyways," Nana said. "You look more like you could use some sleep."

"You seriously expect us to sleep after that?" Ned exclaimed.

"What if the ogres come back?" Robin was near panicking.

"We are safe enough from them in here tonight," Nana assured her, putting a firm gentle hand on top of her trembling one. "I've got some friends keeping an eye on us. So time to go get some sleep while we can."

"I have like eight thousand things running around in my head right now, which is giving me a headache." Ned held his ice pack to his forehead. "Well, worse of a headache."

"Yes, I can imagine," Nana said. "But you need to go to bed regardless."

Ned blinked his eyes at her.

"If you all go to bed without anymore fuss, I will make cinnamon rolls for breakfast."

Well, in that case. "Deal!" Mac and Ned agreed.

After all, fairy tales could turn out to be true, and ogres storm the house, but Nana's cinnamon rolls were definitely worth the risk.

The next day opened with Nana's cinnamon rolls, as promised. Of course, this was after an entire night that had alternated between insomnia and nightmares.

Despite the evening's revelations swarming in his head, Ned fell asleep quickly, although it was a very restless sleep. Monsters chased him through his dreams, and he would jerk awake, only to fall back asleep into another frustrating struggle dream. He was always reading the wrong book and couldn't figure out where the book he wanted was. He was running late for something, despite all his precautions to avoid being late. And the stupid derivative on the chalkboard just wouldn't work the way it was supposed to. When he finally woke to the smell of baking cinnamon, he felt more tired than when he had gone to bed.

"I would ask you how you slept, but your face kind of says it all," Nana said. "Have a seat and dig into the coffee. You're going to need it."

Mac and Robin joined them as Ned poured himself a cup of coffee, trying to clear the fog in his brain. Unsurprisingly, Robin looked worse than Ned did, moving like a zombie and yawning every ten seconds. Mac hummed as she skipped down the stairs and into the kitchen, bouncing from foot to foot with a disturbing amount of energy. But this was also not surprising.

Of course, Mac had slept well, Ned smiled to himself, *probably having wonderful, fantastic, exciting dreams.* Because nothing ever fazed Mac. She was actually excited at the prospect of getting attacked by ogres.

"What exactly are we looking for?" Mac

asked as they entered the library to begin their search.

"Forget the old legends and fairy tales," Nana said. "We're looking for something much more recent. Neighborhood legends. News articles. Social media. Anything about anybody doing anything with an axe that seems out of place, supernatural. With any luck, one of those will be our axe."

"So, how does that work exactly?" Ned asked, picking up the book Nana had handed him last night. "You're saying all these fairy tales are true?"

"Almost every story is rooted in truth, Ned," Nana said. "Knowing to what degree it is twisted by the one telling it, or changed over time throughout history, is the challenge. To be more specific in answer to your question, yes, each of those stories is rooted in something true. Beanstalks are not the only doorway between the worlds. And the beanstalk was around for a long time before Thumbling took over the kingdom. Other things have also been portals throughout history: literal doors and windows, mirrors, even storms."

Mac gave an incredulous smile. "You mean like Alice in *Through the Looking Glass*?"

Nana nodded. "Something like that. Some doors are busier and more traveled than others. The beanstalk here was actually quite busy. Many of the kingdom's people came to live here, staying in touch with friends and family on the other side, trading back and forth.

"Now, once in a while, objects or people will make their way through those portals into our world that are not necessarily special in their world, but once they get here they... do things, becoming the inspiration for many of our legends and fairy tales. A magic shoe made of glass. A mirror that will show you whatever you want. A flute with hypnotic power. Whether the legends come close to the actual truth..." Nana shrugged.

"So, where do we start?" Mac pursed her lips.

"Fetch y'all's computers, will you, dear?" Nana asked Robin while Mac and Ned began brainstorming a list of places to search.

Which actually turned out to be more of Mac's ideas than Ned's. Her excitement kept her almost giddy as her brain worked faster than her hands, resulting in a very hastily scribbled list that only she could read.

"Okay," Mac said as Robin returned, "we've got social media – Facebook, Twitter, Instagram.

YouTube. Blogs. Online newspapers."

"I'll take the newspapers," Robin said, opening her laptop and logging in.

"Okay. I'll put your name next to that."

"Start with the local ones," Nana said as she poured herself a cup of coffee. "Then work your way out. There's no telling how far this thing may have travelled."

"Mac, why don't you and I split up the social media?" Ned said.

"You don't have social media," Mac snorted.

"I have Facebook," Ned objected.

"Which you're hardly ever on."

"You don't have an Instagram?" Robin looked up.

"Fine. If you don't want my help, you take the social media. I'll take YouTube and blogs."

Three sets of fingers flew across three different laptops, and the cyber chase was on. Mac had her hands full balancing two different social media accounts on her computer and one on her phone. Ned dug out his headphones and gritted his way through endless commercials and previews in order to actually watch videos that might contain something of interest. He had to turn the brightness of the screen as low as possible and wear sunglasses to keep from aggravating his concussion. Robin started with the *Houston Chronicle* and searched for any news articles involving axes from Houston and the surrounding areas. Nana kept them well supplied with coffee and snacks, while offering guidance and suggestions.

"What have you got so far, Robin?" Nana asked, planting a kiss on her granddaughter's head and delivering some freshly popped popcorn.

"Um, homeowner shoots and kills axe-wielding intruder who threatens family. A guy who sells memorial axes to fireman. A man in southeast Houston slays his roommate with an axe."

"Wow, you certainly got the depressing part," Ned said.

"Yeah," Robin sighed. "Not much helpful. I'll keep looking."

"So, if this is such an important magical axe," Mac mused, "how'd Ned get a hold of it?"

Nana shrugged and raised her eyebrows. "That I don't know. I'd be interested in finding out though." She sat back and pursed her lips. "The axe was part of a matching set, a sword and an axe, that both had the ability to cut through anything. They had changed hands many times, traversing from world to world, but at the time that Thumbling took over, they were held by the king of Up Root. The sword is in Thumbling's possession now. He'll be wanting the axe because, aside from modern artillery, it is the only weapon that can match the sword."

"What's so special about an axe that can cut through anything?" Robin asked.

"Well, if you think about it," Ned said, leaning back and closing his eyes to have some relief from the light, "you'd always be able to cut through someone's armor. Anything? You'd be able to chop through a tank. Topple buildings. Before the development of machine guns and modern warfare, an axe like that could make you the most powerful man on the battlefield."

Mac tapped her chin. "Maybe… Maybe, we need to focus on the day you were found."

"Robin, could you see if there are any news articles from around that time?"

"You do realize that to go into the archives I'm going to have to buy memberships at a lot of these newspapers?" Robin said. "And not the cheap ones either."

"Use my credit card," Nana said, handing over her purse.

"Nana, we need to talk to whoever was there that day," Ned said.

"The firemen and EMTs." Nana drummed her fingers on her chin. She went to a filing cabinet in the corner and pulled out a small file.

"What about witnesses?" Mac asked. "I mean, if a whole bunch of people had just come through the beanstalk, surely there were some of them still around?"

"And raise questions as to what all of them were doing that deep in the woods during a thunderstorm?" Nana clucked her tongue. "The existence of the beanstalk had been kept hidden by the Up Root community that used it to travel back and forth. No, they scattered pretty quickly once 911 was called. It would be hard to know who most of them were, but I might be able to track a few of them down. I'll make some phone calls. You can start with this. It has a few newspaper clippings from around that time. I believe the EMTs are listed in your hospital paperwork in there as well."

Ned flipped the folder open. "'UFO Boy Appears in National Forest'," he read aloud. "Joy. I always wondered where that nickname came from."

"Well, look on the bright side: now you get to talk to the reporter who started it," Mac grinned.

He was the first person that Ned called.

Mac worked on tracking down the EMTs to see if they were still working. The conversation with the reporter proved to be pretty fruitless. Finally, Ned began to have a few choice words with him.

Robin and Mac looked at each other and smothered their smiles.

"How'd it go?" Mac asked.

"Uh, he hung up."

"I've got a few more names to try. I was able to find some of the EMTs through Facebook, and they're still working here in the area. I was thinking about going to see a few of them in person."

"That sounds like a great idea," Ned nodded. "We could bring some of Nana's cookies and see if that helps."

"Mac and I will," Nana corrected, returning to the room as she hung up the call with whomever she had been talking. "*You* are in no condition to go driving around town. Doctor's orders."

Ned sighed, although he knew it was true. He could already feel the fatigue and the headache setting in anew.

"You get some rest for a little bit. Looking at that computer screen probably isn't doing anything for your concussion. We'll regroup and go over what we've learned when we get back."

Mac planted a kiss on his cheek. "We're bound to learn something! Nana won't let us come back empty handed."

Ned watched through the windows as Nana's truck rolled down the gravel drive. He sure hoped she was right.

6

THE STORM
THICKENS

"SO, WHERE DOES ALL this leave us?" Mac asked.

"Exactly where we were," Ned said.

An exhausted Mac and Nana didn't get home until eight o'clock on their first day of interviews. Ned and Robin were just as exhausted. Robin's eyes were sore from staring at her computer all day long, and she had begun spending more and more of her time staring out the windows or at her phone than her computer. Ned's concussion was still making him feel tired, even after napping on and off throughout the day. All the thoughts and frustrations and wonderings swirling around in his head weren't helping matters. The second day of interviews and research proved to be just as fruitless, so they sought the best remedy they knew. Tea and Nutella in the library.

Mac, trying to be optimistic, wasn't put down so easily. "We just need to keep looking," she said as she dug her spoon back into her jar of Nutella.

"How long do we have before an angry horde of ogres descends upon us?" Ned asked, giving his own spoonful a lick.

"Who knows?" Nana watched the rain trickle down the outside of the windowpanes.

"Horde," Mac echoed. "Nice. I like it."

Ned gave a tired smile. Trust Mac to remain cheerful and try to lighten things up. "I suppose we could just get out Nana's shotgun collection."

"Ah-ha," Nana lowered her mug from her mouth. "I only have the one, dear. But I believe there are a few crossbows and a revolver."

"Crossbows? Dude! How come I didn't know about these sooner?" Ned demanded.

"Probably because of the numerous trips to

the emergency room I had to take you on," Nana snorted. "I wasn't going to give you even more ways to hurt yourself. Although in hindsight, I guess it would have been handy to train you before letting you use them to fight off ogres."

"Can we go take a look?" Mac asked, eyes glowing.

Nana chuckled. "As long as it will lift those long faces and you don't hurt yourselves."

Mac and Ned followed Nana up the stairs, leaving Robin on the couch staring silently into her mug. Buried in the bottom of Nana's closet, behind racks of clothes and shoes, was an old wooden chest locked with a padlock.

"I always wondered what was in there," Ned said as he watched Nana produce the key and unlock it.

"How did you know about it?" Nana narrowed her eyes, her face threatening to turn into full-on interrogation mode.

Ned felt his face get a little red as he gave a sheepish grin. "There may – or may not – have been a few search parties in your closet. What? We knew it was where you hid our Christmas presents."

"Hmmm, that explains a few things," Nana muttered, turning and flipping open the lid.

From the top, Nana pulled a pair of revolvers, the kind you typically think of cowboys wearing. Beneath those were a set of pistol crossbows and an assortment of knives and daggers.

"Where did all this come from?" Mac asked, taking one of the revolvers and opening the empty cylinder.

"A few things I put away, in the odd chance they'd be needed," Nana said. "Some of them are family heirlooms I just couldn't bring myself to get rid of. Like those revolvers. They belonged to my granddaddy. The daggers and crossbows I've collected from various places. I guess we know where Ned gets his affinity for weapons from."

"What about the knives?" Ned asked, sorting through them. There were at least a dozen, each a different make and style, from a Japanese throwing star to a rusty bowie knife. "Looks like the humidity isn't treating this one well."

"What can I say? I've got a thing for knives," Nana chuckled. "I suppose now that you're older, although not much less accident prone, I should bring them out more often. Times are a-changing. Who knows what's going to happen next."

"Doorbell! Pizza's here!"

"I'll go get the door." Mac started to get up

from the floor.

"No, no, you two stay," Ned said, putting a hand on her shoulder. "I can get it."

"Are you sure? How's the head? And the ribs?"

"I've been sitting for most of the day. I need to stretch."

Ned hurried down the stairs as quickly as his injured body would allow to receive the cheesy goodness from the Domino's pizza deliverer.

"Pizza time, Robin!" he said, brandishing the stack of pizza boxes as he entered the library to pass through to the kitchen.

But Robin wasn't where they had left her on the sofa. Or in the kitchen.

He found the note propped up on the bookcase in the entryway as he returned to go back up the stairs. It was labeled only as "Sorry" in Robin's handwriting. Deep down inside, he had a sinking feeling that he already knew what it was going to say. Part of him wanted to rip the paper open while another part of him froze. If he didn't open it, he couldn't read it, and it wouldn't be real. With shaking fingers, he unfolded the piece of paper.

I'm sorry, were the first two words.

But I don't think I can stay. I guess it's every girl's dream to live in a fairy tale. But now that it's real, I don't think I can take it. I'm sorry I can't stay and help. Love y'all. Goodbye.

Ned threw open the front door, even though he knew it was probably too late. "Robin!" he screamed out into the night, ignoring the pain that screamed through his chest when he did. Sheets of rain drowned out his voice and slammed into him as he ran out on the driveway. Robin's car wasn't there.

He hurried back inside, slamming the door shut and staggering up the stairs.

"What is it?" Mac asked, setting down a small box wrapped in tissue paper that she had been going to open.

But Ned's breathing was coming too hard to answer, and he held his arm against his throbbing chest as he wordlessly handed the now-soggy note to Nana.

As she read it, Nana's face fell, and she pressed her lips together. Several times, she looked as though she were about to speak. "Just as well," she said finally. "Best to let her go for now. If we don't find that axe, she'll be safer out there than she will be with us." She handed the letter to Mac.

"But – " Ned's voice cracked. He knew Nana was probably right, *but*...

"She has money. She has her dorm room. She has a car. It's not like she's on the street." Nana's voice was calm and shaky at the same time, the logical side of her trying to reassure the emotional side of her.

The ache wracked up in Ned's chest, and he left the room. Downstairs, he stood in the entryway. His hands shook, and his chest heaved, reminding him with every breath of the bruised ribs from the ogres' attack. The attack that had turned his world upside down. And now it had stolen Robin from him. He tried to reassure himself with Nana's words, repeating them to himself.

She had money. And Nana could always put more into her bank account. She had a dorm room. She had a place to sleep. She had a car. But the oil tended to leak... he should have checked it the other day. He hoped she remembered to check it.

Ned wandered aimlessly into the library and sank onto the sofa. Abandoned on the table where he and Robin usually did puzzles were notepads, folders, and laptops scattered haphazardly like the thoughts in his brain, everything he was still trying to grasp, understand, and come to terms with. So far, their search had turned up nothing, which put them back at square one. More like the square root of negative one, searching for an imaginary axe.

He drifted off to sleep, listening to the rain and wind howl outside.

When he woke up, it was still storming. Someone had covered him with one of Nana's quilts during the night. He checked his phone: 8:00 a.m.

Rolling off the couch, he was reminded how uncomfortable it is to sleep in jeans. The kitchen was empty. No one else was awake. Why should they be? Ned brewed himself some coffee and stared at the deluge outside. Brilliant forks lit up the sky for a split second before the deep boom of thunder rattled the windows. The lights in the kitchen contemplated whether or not to go out, and Ned gave a worried glance up at the light fixtures in the ceiling.

Steam rose out of his coffee mug in front of him as he sat down at the kitchen table and stared at the wall. The only sound besides the rain was the grandfather clock ticking away in the next room.

He wondered how Robin was. He had tried calling and texting her, but she had never answered. He wondered how Nana was holding up. Mac – he was sorry she was caught up in this danger. Thinking of which, where could that stupid magical axe have gone? It's not like axes can disappear into thin air. Then again, maybe they did. This was a magical axe they were talking about.

His wonderings finally ran themselves out, and his mind drifted into silence. The grandfather clock broke the silence by announcing that it was now 9:00. Mac wandered wordlessly into the kitchen and headed straight for the coffee. Sitting across the table from Ned, she gave him a half smile in greeting.

"Thanks for the blankets," Ned spoke first as Mac sipped her coffee.

"Sleep okay?"

Ned shrugged. "You?"

"Fine."

"And Nana? How's she holding up?" Ned asked.

"I can't really tell," Mac said.

"And what about you?"

"If I wasn't doing okay, trust me: you would know."

Would he? Ned accepted her answer. For now. "I don't think any of us are going to get out in this weather. I guess we've got a lot more internet searching to do."

"Careful, the NSA might start to wonder about you."

Ned chortled, spewing coffee back into his mug. Just as he recovered, the electricity decided to officially go out.

Ned and Mac stared at each other across the darkness.

Wonderful. "Well, scratch that," Ned said.

With the storm raging and the electricity out, there wasn't much research they could do. While Nana read some books, Mac and Ned worked on a puzzle. It helped give Ned something to focus on besides the puzzle in his head, the mystery of himself, the problem of the axe.

The storm eventually faded, but the electricity still didn't come back on, and there was still plenty of water on the roads. Nana drifted into the kitchen and disappeared. Mac browsed Nana's shelves, pulling out books at random and flipping through them. Ned bent over the book that Nana had first shown them with the illustration of the ogres. Curious how some of the stories differed somewhat from the traditional versions that he knew.

He fell asleep trying to make it through an alternate version of "Rip Van Winkle", which wasn't an improvement over the one he had been forced to read for high school literature. When he woke up, it was mid-afternoon, and the electricity had come back on at some point. From the smell of it, Nana had been stress baking. Her cooking efforts had produced the fantastic smell of banana bread and cookies, so he decided to try his luck in the kitchen. Mac was fast asleep at the kitchen table, surrounded by a pile of Nana's weapons and a few other interesting looking objects. He didn't want to wake her, so he helped himself to a good snack and went back to the library.

Without the storm pounding all around them outside, the house was eerily silent. Piles of books surrounded him. Notepads, lists of ideas, tries and failures, newspaper articles. Ned felt claustrophobia press down on him, overwhelmed by it all. All his thoughts. All the worrying of the last three days. The axe. Robin.

He needed to get out. Abandoning the stack of freshly buttered banana bread, Ned headed for the entryway. Mac woke up and found him putting on his boots and helmet.

"What's going on?" she yawned. "Where ya

goin'?"

"I just need some air, some space to go clear my head," Ned said as he pulled on his gloves. "I'm just going for a ride." Before Mac could protest, Ned bolted out the door and headed for his bike.

The storm had brought in a cool front, and the open air felt refreshing after being trapped in the house the last few days. As always, his head started to clear as soon as his bike reached the end of the driveway. Just the road and the wind. Nothing to do but focus on driving. And Walmart. He could go for some Blue Bell ice cream and stretch his legs. He ate out of the gallon tub of cookies and cream as he walked through the store, not really caring about the looks he received. It was Walmart – what were people expecting anyways?

Hmmmm, was that a metal detector? Well, that was interesting... actually, that was an idea... He pulled the box off the shelf. Meh, he could go for that price; not like they had any other ideas.

An hour later, he was walking in a circular pattern around a familiar clearing in the woods, sweeping the metal detector from side to side. The rains had turned most of the woods into a swamp, something he hadn't thought about before he parked at the trailhead. Thick sticky mud covered the parts of the ground that weren't miniature lakes. Ankle deep layers of pine needles, ferns, and bracken helped to provide a little bit more solid footing here and there.

Trying not to think about how hard it was going to be to clean off his boots, he went meticulously at first, slowly passing over every square inch of dirt, then as his search continued to turn up nothing, he lazily swung the detector back and forth. As the sun started going down, he was forced to walk back to the parking lot, call Mac, and ask her to come out with a flashlight. She met him at the trailhead thirty minutes later, armed with a headlamp, a battery powered lantern, and a relieved expression.

"I was getting worried," she said climbing out of Nana's truck and giving him a hug. "Don't go driving off like that, please."

Ned hugged her back, kissing the top of her head. "I'm sorry. I just really had to get out. And then, I had an idea." He held up the metal detector. "Not really the most brilliant thing. Probably a waste of time."

"No, that's about the best thing we've got going right now." Mac handed him a can of bug spray. "But I'm not going in there without this."

"Bless you," Ned kissed her forehead again.

"Just what I was needing, besides an axe."

They stumbled through the woods, down the small unofficial trail that Ned knew all too well, to the place where his life as far back as he could remember had started. Where he had been found after being struck by lightning. And as he now knew, the location of the original beanstalk. He had come back to it many times when he was younger, hoping to recover any of the memories that he had lost.

"I'm not even sure how much longer I'm going to keep this up," Ned sighed. "I'm fixing to give it up as another dumb idea." He kicked at a root in frustration, then slapped at a mosquito.

"You okay?" Mac asked.

"A few days ago, my biggest concern in life was passing business cal this semester. And now I'm in the middle of the woods, wandering around in the dark, in the mud, looking for a magical axe, so I can defeat an angry giant from another world. I found out that I'm also from this other world, and pretty much everything about my life is a lie. My sister just ran away. And to top it all off, I was beaten up by a gang of ogres. Other than that, I'm okay."

"Not everything about your life is a lie," Mac assured him gently squeezing his hand. "I'm not."

Ned held onto her hand and sighed. "I know. Thanks, Mac."

They stood in silence for a few minutes listening to the crickets and the frogs and the wind rustling through the trees.

"I do hope you're not just going to stand there all night."

7

DO WE HAVE A
DEAL?

NED WAS GLAD HE wasn't the only one who jumped. The voice came from above their heads, so he and Mac both shined their lights upwards into the trees. The light bounced off of two glowing eyes. A cat crouched in the tree branches above them.

"I mean I love a good silence as much as the next feline, but finding your axe is a little more important at this point."

"It's a talking cat," Ned shrugged.

"You know about the axe?" Mac asked.

Ned's heart had started beating again but was now thumping in his chest like the drummer of a heavy metal band. "Of course, it does." He was surprised at his own calm acceptance of this, which four days ago he would have been totally freaked out by.

"So you still haven't found it," the cat surmised, bounding down on top of a fallen log. "I know someone who can help with that."

"You know someone who knows where to find my axe?"

"More or less." The cat started off through the woods. "Well, are you coming?"

Ned and Mac exchanged glances. "Sure, we're coming. Why not?"

Ned took Mac by the hand and led the way following the cat. Which wasn't easy to do. It stayed about ten feet in front of them and didn't always choose the most direct or clear path, sticking to tree branches and the tops of fallen logs. Ned was jealous that this enabled it to stay clear of the muddy forest floor.

As the trees thinned, the cat dropped to the ground, ducking through the underbrush, and finally led them to the back of a small hut sitting in a clearing.

"Really?" the cat snapped. "We're going to

do this? Turn your face to me, you stupid excuse for a house, and put your back to the woods!"

Ned felt that he could hardly be surprised by anything else, but he was proven wrong when the hut rose up on stilts and turned to face them before nestling back down in the grass.

"Were those chicken legs?" Ned asked.

"Ghastly sight, aren't they?" the cat agreed with his sentiments.

A dog's face popped up over the top of the garden fence that seemed to have rotated with the house. It disappeared, and then reappeared as the little gate swung open.

"Oh, good, you found them! Oh good. Come in, come in!" He continued to wag his tail vigorously and dance at their feet as he led them to the door of the cottage. "We've been waiting for you," he said over his shoulder, bouncing into the hut.

"We?" Mac echoed.

Her question was answered by a curious, ancient, old woman hunched over a walking cane. "We," she said in a heavy Eastern European accent, turning from stirring a small pot on a stove with a wooden spoon. "And is about time," she glared over her spectacles. "Have seat."

"Uh, no thanks," Ned shook his head. "Who

are you?"

"Sit!"

Two seats flew from out of nowhere, scooped them up from behind, and plunked down in front of a round wooden table. To their left, a fireplace with a cast iron insert crackled cheerfully under a wooden mantel. On top of the mantel was a curious collection of small boxes, about the size of jewelry boxes. There were different kinds made of different metals and woods. A few were inlaid with mosaics of decorative tiles. Behind them was a large wooden cabinet with cookbooks and a collection of dishes, some porcelain, some silver, some crystal. A wooden settee with floral patterned cushions and a carved back sat across the room from them. The room itself was not very wide. The kitchen was to their right. It was a hodgepodge of various cabinets, drawers, a stove, and a refrigerator all crammed into the tiny space, barely leaving room for the kitchen sink and a steep narrow staircase leading to a loft above them. Kettles and frying pans, dried herbs and other bundles, hung from the rafters collecting cobwebs.

"You're a witch?" Mac guessed.

"How very astute of you, Mackenzie," the woman said dryly. "My name is Babba Ygga."

"Like the *John Wick* movie?" Ned frowned.

"You don't quite look like what I would have expected."

"We've had to change appearances," the witch said. "Back in day, if people saw you, they'd be terrified. I remember screams. Quite useful, that fear. But problem nowadays, you either get people asking where you buy costume and tell you is so 'cool', or they snap picture and post on internet with caption 'world ugliest woman'. Not so useful. So, yes, we make adjustments." She brushed a wisp of hair back from her face. Indeed, she seemed to be such an ordinary old woman. Thick silver hair twisted into a bun at the back of her head. A pair of glasses rested on her wrinkled face, and she wore a blue jean apron over a simple blue cotton dress and a pink sweater.

But it was her eyes that were unnerving, unnaturally dark and sly, watching them as a tiger does when it's deciding whether or not to consider you its prey. Ned shuddered to think how the screams of terrified villagers back in the day had been useful.

"And you must be Jack."

"Actually, I go by Ned... now." It felt strange to be addressed as "Jack". Ned wasn't sure how he felt about it.

"So you do. But that doesn't change fact you still looking for axe, but you can't remember where it is."

"Your cat told us you knew where to find it," Ned said cautiously. Just because he was curious about whether or not she *could* help him, it didn't mean it would be a good idea to *let* her help him.

Perched on a mantle above the fireplace, the tabby looked up briefly, then went back to cleaning the mud off of itself as it purred.

"Of course; well, more or less. That's why she brought you here."

"So, where is it?"

"In your head."

"I think I'd know if there was an axe sticking out of my head."

"No, I mean I don't have to tell you where axe is. You were there. You saw it. All we have to do is help you remember."

"And how are you going to do that? By looking into your crystal ball?"

Babba Ygga waved her wooden spoon and snorted. "Typical ignorance. Crystal balls are for looking into future, depending on crystal. Not exact science, and very, how do you say? Unreliable. No, we are going to use tea." She dipped a ladle into the pot she had been stirring and poured its content into a cup.

"You want me to drink that? And I just magically remember where the axe is?"

"Basically."

"And you're offering to help me why?"

"Is not that simple," the witch waved her finger, sitting down across from him. "I want something in return."

"What? Money?"

"No. A favor."

"You want a favor from us?" Mac's eyes went wide. "Ned, this is a bad idea."

"Of course, it is," Ned agreed. "What kind of favor?"

"I want you to bring something to me. Somewhere, sometime, in not-so-distant future, you will come across items of great value. You will bring them to me."

"What kind of item?"

"Details," the witch waved her hand. "We get to that later."

"What kind of item?" Ned pushed again.

"Is not weapon if that's what you worry about," the witch said.

"Anything can be used as a weapon," Ned countered, holding the witch's gaze.

"You are true," she conceded. "They are three small golden leaves. Nothing more, nothing less."

"And how do you know I will find them?"

"Crystal ball," the witch said, clucking her tongue. "Obviously. Now, do we have a deal?"

Three golden leaves? It seemed such a small price to pay in order to save the world. But appearances can be deceiving. Ned knew there was probably more to the leaves than she was letting on. But he reached for the cup anyways, curious as to what was in it.

He sniffed suspiciously, but his hesitation was not for reasons that he had expected. "What kind of tea is this?"

"Mint, Vitamin D, with few other special ingredients. Is incredibly good for memory, and did you know that is also recommended for people studying for exams? You chew mint gum while studying, then you chew during exam. Helps trigger memory. I have special infused stock if you are interested. $10 bag."

"I'm allergic to mint," Ned said, setting the cup back down on the table.

Babba Ygga peered at him over her spectacles. "How allergic?"

"Like I'mma-need-an-EpiPen allergic."

"That does present problem," Babba Ygga said, taking off her spectacles.

"No kidding. Do you know how difficult it is to find toothpaste? I have to brush my teeth with baking soda half the time."

"This could explain why you never remember before," Babba Ygga nodded. "However, there are only three ways for me to help you. One way, well, is impossible if you want to stay alive. Out of other two, this one is least dangerous." She rose and took a large plastic medicine box off the top of a cabinet. "So question you have is: just how badly you want to find axe?" She pulled an EpiPen out of the box and held it out to him.

Ned took it, slowly, contemplating, trying to steady his nervous breathing. He was desperate, and unfortunately, the witch knew that. Frustration tore him up inside. Frustration with this witch, with the axe, that he couldn't remember, with Nana even. And frustration and desperation were a dangerous combination. He stared into the cup in front of him. "You saw me in the future? That means I'm going to survive all of this, right?"

"If you don't get yourself killed, that is what will happen. There are many paths between now and then. Do we have a deal?" Babba Ygga asked again.

Ned made up his mind. There were worse ways to go. And he'd probably made worse decisions before. "Get ready," he said handing the EpiPen to Mac. Before she could protest or say anything, he downed the cup, choking and spluttering as he got near the end. Hopefully, it wouldn't take long.

8

FROM THE DEPTHS OF MEMORY

IT WAS HARD TO tell dream from reality. Visions danced in Ned's head, but he knew somewhere that Mac and Babba Ygga were leaning over him. He knew he was lying on a hard wooden floor, but everything above him looked like a forest. Instead of Mac and Babba Ygga, he saw a dark sky, occasionally streaked with lightning. He could feel the sensation of raindrops landing on his face. Somewhere in the background, a man was talking in a low voice.

Ned could just see the glint of an axe to his right out of the corner of his eye. He tried to reach for it, but his body would not respond. Above him, there was a woman's face, blurry and indistinct, but oh-so-familiar, leaning over him.

"Jack," she whispered, tears in her eyes. "Jack, can you hear me? Stay with me, baby."

"They're on their way," the man's voice cut in. "You need to leave now."

The woman glanced over her shoulder then turned back to Ned. "I am so sorry, Jack, but I have to go. They'll be coming for you, Jack. They'll find you soon enough. I love you."

"Time to go!" The man's voice was becoming more urgent.

The woman picked up the axe but could not take her eyes off of Ned. "I wish I had more time. I wish I could keep you with me. But this is the only way I know to protect you," she said. "You will find me when it's time. The enchanted garden. Come and find me." The woman looked over her shoulder. "I have to go," she said again. "I'll be waiting at the enchanted garden!"

Ned wanted to scream at her as she stood up, to wait, come back, what garden? But as she disappeared from his vision, Ned heard a loud din of fire trucks in the distance, the low buzz of four wheelers coming towards him, lights flashing back and forth through the forest, and then there were people's faces over him.

Mac and Babba Ygga's faces broke through his dream, the flashing lights were replaced by the fireplace behind them, and the engine noises turned out to be the cat purring right next to his head. The raindrops were the little dog, who was standing next to his head and licking his face.

He was still lying on the floor, and every time he tried to take a breath, it felt as if an elephant was sitting on his chest. That could have been caused by the aftereffects of an allergic reaction and anaphylactic shock, or by the cat sitting there staring into his face and purring, rising up and down with each of Ned's struggled breaths.

Mac's and the witch's faces both showed relief as Ned blinked up at them in recognition.

"Oh, you're alive," Mac sighed in relief. She collapsed forward for a moment, resting her head on the cat on Ned's chest.

"You do have way of surprising world and cheating death, Master Jack," Babba Ygga leaned back and pushed strands of white hair out of her face. "Maybe there's some hope for world yet. Lie still and rest for moment. Catch your breath. You, *eedtee!*" she chided the cat, muttering something else in Russian.

Mac lifted her head as the cat sidled off of Ned's chest. "How do you feel?" she asked anxiously, a hint of tears in her voice.

"That's going to hurt," Ned managed to gasp. Breathing grew easier, but his hands were shaking from the adrenaline rush, the shock, and the epinephrine.

"We need to get you to a hospital!"

"No, no, no time for that." Ned tried to roll over, but his trembling body still wouldn't move like he wanted. "We need to go get the axe."

"It worked?!" Mac asked in surprise.

"Sort of." Ned tried to remember what the woman had said. The garden. The enchanted garden?

"Open up." Babba Ygga shoved a maple-flavored sugary object into his mouth.

Almost instantly, Ned felt calmer and steadier. He tucked it under his tongue and waited for the effects to increase. "Wow, this is really good."

"Wait until it dissolves, and then you should be good to go. Just don't go swimming for hour."

"Well, I don't plan on swimming," Ned

shook his head, rolling over and pushing himself into a kneeling position. "Then again, there's a lot of things I didn't plan on."

Within the hour, they were back at Nana's truck. After much arguing, Ned rode home on his bike with Mac following him to make sure he would be alright. Ned didn't care what condition he was in – he wasn't going to leave his bike at the trailhead overnight. But the witch's pill seemed to have worked its magic for now. His head felt clearer than it had for days, and his ribs didn't hurt anymore either.

Ned's phone buzzed in his pocket as they walked up to the door. "I hope that's not Nana. She has enough to worry about."

"Wait until she finds out you traded a favor to the Russian equivalent of the boogey man," Mac snorted.

"Ah, she doesn't need to know about that… yet." Ned raised a finger for emphasis. Of course, Nana would probably find out eventually. But she had enough stress right now. Besides, he might not live long enough to even have to worry about delivering on his end of the deal. Odd how that thought seemed to cheer him up.

He didn't recognize the number calling, but he had two previous missed calls from it in the last hour. "Hello?" he yawned.

"Ned Parker?" the voice on the other end asked.

Ned tipped his head back in frustration. Too many random people looking for him and wanting something from him. "Depends on who's calling."

"Roddy Kennedy." No wonder the voice had sounded familiar.

"Great. You should know I'm not in the mood."

"Before you hang up, I'm just trying to warn you," Roddy said in a low voice. "They've got Robin."

"Who?" Ned asked, already knowing the answer. For the third time that night, he felt as though he were going to have a heart attack.

"My cousins."

Ned combed his fingers through his hair in frustration. "What have they done to her, and where the heck is your uncle?"

"She's fine. I've been able to keep them in check for now. Uncle Fergus has been out all day. Searching for your axe. He's not answering his phone."

Ned stopped in surprise. Although, he really shouldn't have been. Mr. Kennedy had already known about it. "So, why would you tell us?" Ned asked. "Did you call the cops?"

"I'm a wolf. I'm not stupid."

Ned nearly strangled himself holding back a scream of frustration. Were there any other surprises he should be aware of? "I'm sorry, did you say 'wolf'?"

"More like a werewolf. If the police show up, things could get... complicated."

Ned resigned himself to the fact that there was always going to be something new that somebody had neglected to tell him. "I'm coming."

"Need the address?"

"Nope."

"You'll need the gate code: 3175."

"I'll let you know when I'm there."

Ned hung up the phone and barged through the door, tossing his helmet to the side. It was a habit that Nana hated, but he was more than a little annoyed with her at the moment, so she was just going to have to put up with it.

"Ned, what's going on?" Mac asked in a calm-but-I'm-about-to-go-ballistic-on-you voice.

"Fergus took Robin," Ned said, rummaging through a closet in the hallway. "I'm going to get her back."

"Is she – I'm coming with!"

"No, Mac, I need you to stay here with Nana. Don't tell her what's going on."

"So help me, if Fergus has done *anything*," Mac growled.

"He's not going to get the chance." Ned's hands finally grasped what they sought. A heavy-duty metal baseball bat.

"I'm curious. Did you have a plan, besides barging in with a baseball bat?" Roddy asked coolly.

"I'm sorry. I was going to tell you, but I was waiting for the sarcasm to start giving suggestions."

Ned crouched behind a massive tangle of shrubbery watching the Kennedy family home. The approach to the house was much longer and more secluded than Nana's, and he had left his motorcycle at the gates so as to avoid the noise. The mansion lay at the end of a half mile gravel drive sheltered by stately rows of pine trees, well lit by lampposts and lights all over the exterior of the house. Ned had never been inside the gates but had passed by the house many times before, figuring it would come in handy someday to know exactly where Fergus lived.

Ned did have a plan. Sort of. Not that it was a very good plan…

On the other end of the phone call, Roddy grunted. "My apologies. What is your plan?"

"I'll be the distraction. I need you to get her out."

"Look, Parker, if my cousins find out I helped you – "

"I'll never be able to get in there," Ned said. "Not by myself. Why did you bother calling if you're not going to help?"

Roddy started to say something but stopped and sighed. Ned could almost hear the internal struggle Roddy was having as he argued with himself inside his head.

"Okay, Jack," he finally conceded in a tight strangled voice.

"Don't call me that," Ned gritted his teeth.

"Don't do anything stupid."

9

BAD WOLF

ROBIN JUMPED A LITTLE as the door opened, even though she had been waiting for it. Gripping the rectangular porcelain toilet lid with sweaty shaking hands, she had tried to prepare herself to smash whoever came through that door next, but now she stood half-frozen in fear, unable to bring her arms over her head.

Roddy slid through the door, holding his arm up in front of him as a shield, hinting that he had been expecting her and her brandished weapon.

Robin relaxed slightly, almost relieved in spite of herself. Roddy had been the only civil person in the entire Kennedy house when Fergus and his brothers had dragged her in and locked her in an upstairs bedroom. Roddy was the one who had forced his cousins to bring her food, even eating with her to prove the food wasn't drugged. She got the impression all the others were intimidated by him, and that that had served as her protection. Still, she didn't completely trust him. She hugged her porcelain shield against her shaking body.

"You need to come with me," he said.

Her body froze, and she shook her head, shrinking away from him.

"Robin, I know you're scared, but you have to trust me. We need to go right now."

Robin took another step back, reluctant to relinquish the safety of having her toilet lid between herself and anybody else.

"Ned's waiting outside. Come look out the window, and I'll show you." Roddy turned his back to her and left the room.

After hesitating a moment, she peeked round the doorway to make sure no one was waiting to surprise her, then she tiptoed after him to the window at the end of the hall. It overlooked the front of the house, and as they stood there, a familiar figure on a motorcycle came roaring up the drive.

"Ned," she wailed in relief.

"Come on." Roddy took her by the hand and turned to go back down the hallway.

Robin slammed into him as he came to a sudden stop. Looking around him, she saw why. Joel Kennedy, Fergus' younger brother, was down the hall at the top of the stairs.

"What's goin' on, Roddy? Trying to keep her all to yourself?"

Roddy didn't answer. Through the window, they could hear muffled shouts and insults being exchanged.

Ned ground his motorcycle to a halt, spraying gravel over the brick patio.

"Kennedy!" he roared through his helmet. "Where is she?"

"Well, look who finally decided to join the party." Fergus rose from the deck chairs where he and Declan Kennedy had been lounging under the porch lights

"Where is she?" Ned demanded again.

"Watch it, do you want to get beat up again?" Fergus chided, waving at Ned with the beer bottle in his hand.

For an answer, Ned pulled a chunk of rock from his jacket pocket and heaved it. It smashed through a window, narrowly missing Declan's head.

"Alright, fine. You asked for it." Fergus charged at Ned, only to be met with a smack across his chest from the baseball bat Ned produced.

As Fergus doubled over the motorcycle in pain, Ned spun around to meet Declan, ramming him in the chest with the end of the bat and shoving him backwards. There was a shattering of glass, and Ned felt something whack him as Fergus smashed his beer bottle into Ned's side. In return, Ned delivered another smack in Fergus' ribs with his baseball bat.

Arms grabbed Ned from behind. He wrestled to get out of Declan's grip, and the two of them stumbled around, tripping over a glass and metal framed coffee table on the patio. They fell backwards into a sea of shattering glass. As he was underneath, Declan absorbed most of the impact. Ned rolled and clocked him with an elbow to the nose. Now free, he started to rise.

But all he saw was a mass of fur and teeth before he was knocked back down flat on his back. The wolf had him by the arm that he had thrown up to shield himself. Sharp teeth pierced through his motorcycle jacket, digging into his flesh and shaking him back and forth. While his free arm punched at the wolf's head, Ned's knees and feet drove upward into the wolf's stomach and hind legs. Twisting the baseball bat in his right hand, he brought the bat down hard on the wolf's snout. He couldn't get a good angle, but a strike is a strike. The thrashing wolf turned its head just in time to receive the end of the bat right in the eye.

The wolf let go of Ned's arm and snapped at the bat, seizing it between its massive jaws, jerking it out of Ned's hand, and swinging it at his head. It bounced off of Ned's helmet, but as his head turned to the side under the force of the blow, Ned saw something else on the ground. Grabbing the beer bottle, he shoved it straight up into the wolf's throat. The wolf yelped, hacking and coughing. Now he was able to kick the wolf off.

Roddy motioned to a room on the left side of the hallway. "Get inside and lock the door."

Robin stepped back towards the doorway as Joel charged forward and Roddy swerved to stop him. But what happened next froze her in her tracks. As he leapt through the air, Roddy transformed before her eyes from a human into a wolf. And it was no longer Joel but another wolf meeting Roddy head on. The two wolves collided, scrambling around on the floor, and then tumbled down the stairs, snapping, snarling, biting, and clawing.

Robin ran forward to the top of the stairs. The wolves were below her on the landing, still fighting. Then the banister broke, and they fell straight down the rest of the way. It was hard for her to tell who was who. Now one of them was coming straight up the stairs towards her with its face twisted into a vicious snarl. Then he jerked to a sudden stop as the other wolf caught up to him, snapping onto his tail and stopping him short. The wolf at the top dug deep grooves into the wooden stairs with its claws, trying to move upwards.

Robin's eyes darted between the two wolves. In a moment, she recognized that the other wolf, the one that had appeared where Joel should have been, had more brown. And that was the one at the top of the stairs coming after her.

Almost without realizing she was doing it, she brought her toilet lid down onto the wolf's head. He collapsed, and the other one fell backwards down to the landing.

That wolf scrambled back onto all fours at the landing. "To the back hallway," he growled.

It was Roddy's voice. Robin's overwhelmed, confused, and terrified mind grasped at that one thing out of all the thoughts and questions and fears swirling around inside her head. Roddy was taking her to Ned. She had to follow Roddy.

A roar behind him made Ned scramble to get out of the way. But this wolf was not interested in him. It dove straight for the other wolf. The two wolves snarled and snapped and clawed at each other as they rolled around in the gravel.

Ned pushed himself off the ground and picked up the baseball bat. It took him a moment, but he figured out which wolf had to be Fergus. The brown tinged one still hacking and wheezing. He strode forward and brought the bat down onto Fergus's head. Fergus crumpled to the ground with a pathetic yelp.

Ned turned and saw to his relief a terrified, but otherwise okay, Robin standing in the doorway of the house. Declan was still down on the ground, shrinking away from Ned with one hand held up in surrender while the other tried to stem the flow of blood from his nose.

"Let's go!" Ned yelled, grabbing Robin and pulling her away from the house.

As he scrambled onto the motorcycle and turned the key, Robin climbed on behind and clung to him with trembling arms. The motorcycle roared to life, and they hurtled towards the gates. Roddy joined them, running alongside the motorcycle. They careened down the long drive, spraying gravel and dirt as they went. Wolf and motorcycle dashed out the gates and flew down the back roads, finally bursting out of the woods and roaring straight up Nana's driveway.

Silence descended as he switched the engine off. Ned closed his eyes and breathed a deep sigh of relief. His left arm was throbbing and his heart was still hammering. But that didn't matter. He had Robin. He could feel her trembling behind him.

"You okay?" he asked, removing his helmet and hugging her arms to his chest with his good arm.

"Oh, Ned," she wailed.

He let her sob into his shoulder for a few minutes, cradling her head against his neck. But as relief flooded his bones and the adrenaline rush subsided, he felt himself tilting sideways.

"Whoa, Ned, Ned," Robin gulped, jerking him back upright.

"I'm fine," Ned shook himself, trying to wake himself back up. "Just a flesh wound. I'm sure Mac will love to attack it with some more hydrogen peroxide."

"I think we'd best check out the house."

They both turned to face Roddy, who had changed back into his human form, and was staring past them at the house.

Following his gaze, they looked towards the front door, which stood ajar. But it was the large deep grooves in the door itself that triggered their internal alarm bells.

Ned grabbed his baseball bat and hurried into the house, Roddy and Robin right behind him. The rug in the entryway was twisted and wrinkled across the floor. To their left, the glass panes in the French doors leading into the library were smashed and the doors hung crooked on their hinges. Nearly every bookshelf was emptied, books and torn pages were spread across the floor, and one bookshelf was even tipped over, leaning on its face against the back of the sofa.

It was the eerie silence that chilled Ned the most. "Mac!" he called, his fear of what might have happened to them worse than the fear of whether or not any attackers were still in the house. "Nana!"

A muffled groan from underneath the fallen bookshelf made his blood curdle and his hair stand up on end.

"Nana!" Robin screamed, leaping forward.

Robin tore at the pile of books as Ned and Roddy lifted the shelf and pushed it back against the wall. Nana and her shotgun were underneath. Several large bruises marred her face, and a cut over her eye was dripping blood.

"Nana!" Robin shouted again.

Nana's eyes fluttered open, weakly searching for something to focus on.

"Ned, Ned, they got her," Nana moaned.

"No, Nana, she's right here. Robin's fine."

"Oh, Robin," Nana sighed, her eyes closing.

"Nana, stay awake," Ned said gently but firmly. "Where is Mac?"

Nana's eyes flittered open once more. "I'm so sorry, Ned. I tried to stop them. But they took her."

"Who?" It was Ned's turn to start screaming. He felt the pounding of his heart almost cease altogether.

"The ogres! They took her, Ned." Nana's

voice trailed off and she sank into a dead faint.

10

THE ENCHANTED GARDEN

NED DIDN'T EVEN REMEMBER who called for an ambulance. The three of them followed the ambulance to the hospital in Nana's truck – it was probably Roddy driving. At some point, someone in the emergency room saw Ned's arm and asked if he was okay. They took him back to get it looked at and asked him what bit him.

"Dog."

Was that what had attacked the older lady, they wanted to know.

118

"Don't know. Wasn't there," he replied.

They usually had to say something twice for it to register in his brain.

Nana was going to be okay. She came back to consciousness, but she still needed rest, someone said.

As they sat beside Nana's bed, Ned dozed on and off while Robin slept with her head on his shoulder. He wanted to stay awake for Nana, but he was oh-so-tired. His head was so overwhelmed that everything was turning into one big numb blur.

"You again."

Ned started and turned his head to see Officers Briggs and Dawson standing in the doorway of the hospital room.

"Who... who called you?" he managed to ask.

"Whoever called 911 for an ambulance," Briggs answered. "Dispatch reported a break-in, and given our prior history with that address, my captain sent us up. All things being equal, I'm beginning to wish he hadn't."

Ned nodded numbly. He couldn't blame them.

"You okay, kid?" Dawson asked. "What happened?"

"Another 'gang'," Ned said after a moment.

The two officers exchanged glances.

"I don't even know where to begin with that," Dawson pinched the bridge of his nose.

"It wouldn't have anything to do with them other dumb rich kids that showed up at this same hospital, would it?" Briggs asked.

Ned looked down at his arm, wrapped in gauze and bandages. "In a way…"

"Do you have any idea what these 'gangs' are or what they're after? Can't help if I don't know anything."

And just what were they supposed to help with? Ned had no idea of how to begin. Or did he? Another question rose in his mind, and the dawning of an answer. He pulled his phone out of his pocket, but the battery was dead. So he rose to his feet, waking Robin up, and began rummaging through every single cabinet in the hospital room, without regard to the noise or the mess he was making.

"Can we help you?" Briggs asked.

"I need a *Yellow Pages*," Ned muttered, rummaging through one more cabinet. "Aha!" The pages flew back and forth as he opened the directory book and searched. "I need – I need – ," he said again without bothering to finish his thought. He had found what he needed anyways. "I need you to stay here with them."

"Wait, Ned, where are you going?" Robin cried, grabbing at his jacket as he ran into the hallway.

"I'm going to get the axe," Ned said, kissing her on the forehead.

"Why do I feel like this is something I don't want to hear?" he heard Briggs groan as he turned and left.

The Enchanted Garden wasn't as hard to find as he had expected. He had been so preoccupied with everything having to do with Up Root that he had expected the enchanted garden to literally be a garden that was enchanted. It hadn't occurred to him that it was the name of a plant nursery. The name had rung a bell in the back of his mind, and now that he knew what it was, it made total sense. After getting his phone to charge a little bit on the truck's phone charger, he was able to find it on Google Maps.

The Enchanted Garden was on the southwest side of Houston, nestled in what had once been cotton, rice, and sugar cane growing territory, down country roads past the outskirts of the suburb Sugar Land. The first light of dawn filtered through ancient, majestic pecan trees and live oaks draped lazily in Spanish moss onto a maze of flowers, herbs, bushes, and garden décor.

The gate to the parking lot wasn't open yet, so Ned parked the truck on the side road. Gravel crunched beneath his feet as he walked across the grounds that covered several acres. There was an old house at the front, overgrown with vines climbing up the once-white porch railings. Weeds spilled around everything. The decorative wheelbarrow out front had more dead leaves than potted plants inside it, and the wooden sign swung in the early morning wind, creaking in a most eerie way.

No one answered when he knocked, but the door wasn't even latched. It swung open onto a surprisingly neat shop. Wooden shelves were arranged in neat aisles and piled high with decorative flowerpots and statuettes. Gardening tools and pamphlets on different types of soil, seeds, and mulch lined the shelves. Teapots and paintings adorned the walls. Odd looking bundles hung from the ceiling, bumping his head as he meandered towards the counter.

The counter was neatly arranged with a

variety of merchandise, from keychains to chocolate bars to little potted desk plants. And even little brown packets that looked very familiar. Ned squinted as he leaned in closer. Babba Ygga's mint gum.

"Huh," he chuckled to himself.

"Can I help ya?" A small, brunette, middle-aged woman leaned out of the doorway of an adjacent room.

"Ah," Ned straightened. "Sorry. Were y'all open yet? The door was unlocked."

"I was here anyways, jest goin' through some files. How can I help ya?"

"I'm actually not sure where to begin."

"Perhaps start with whatture lookin' for," the woman suggested in a sweet East Texas twang, coming through the doorway to the counter. "Do ya know?"

"I'm looking for... well, do you carry any axes?"

The woman's eyes narrowed as she scrutinized Ned from head to toe, then widened in realization. "Jack. Jack Ackerman."

"I go by Ned now." Ned felt a little uncomfortable with his new/old name.

"Ya have yer mother's eyes," the woman said, seeming not to hear him. "And 'er face. I'm told ya got yer daddy's hair, but I never knew 'im so I wouldn't know."

Ned stopped, his heart skipping a beat. "You knew my mom?"

"Maggie? Yes, yes, we owned the place together." The woman fetched a framed picture from farther down the counter. A younger version of the woman in front of him and the woman from Ned's vision stood together in front of a much newer looking shop. "She talked 'bout ya a lot. Wonderin' how much ya'd grown and whatcha were goin' to be like. She really hoped to see ya agin someday."

A wave of disappointment washed over Ned. "What happened to her?"

"Disappeared," the woman answered as gently as possible. "Police never did find any sign of 'er. Never knew what happened. It's been over four years now. But she said ya'd be by one day. Or at least, that's what she hoped. She left a letter fer ya. Come on back, and I'll see iffen I can dig it up."

Ned followed the woman into another room. Through a door to his right, he could see out across the grounds. From the furniture, he could tell that the room served as office, kitchen, and breakroom for the woman now rummaging through an old banker's box.

"This is 'er stuff," the woman said apologetically, stopping and looking at Ned. "Didn't know what to do with it at first, but havin' it 'round jest made the hurt worse. Thought it'd be better if I put it outta sight, but I always found myself goin' back and goin' through it all. I guess it'd all be yers now. I'm sorry ya didn't git to see her." Gingerly, she set the box down on the little round pinewood table. "Here's the letter. She always told me that I was s'pposed to give that to ya iffen she weren't around."

Ned sat down in one of the wooden chairs that she offered him. The white envelope gave way to pale purple stationary inside. Unfolding the paper, Ned swallowed hard as he read the cursive handwriting.

My dearest Jack,

If we never meet again, please know that it was because I was trying to protect you. By now, you probably know all about being Jack and where we came from. You should also know, there are dark forces, powerful people, that will never stop looking for that axe – which means they'll be looking for you. I thought the best way to protect you was to keep you hidden, even if that meant that we must live as strangers, and I never got to call you my son again.

Remember, Jack, it is not as important where you came from. What matters more is where you are going. I hope that you will grow to be a fine man, honest and kind and brave. Your choices may very well affect the future of many. Learn from your mistakes.

If you want to find what you're looking for, go down to the river. Take a coin from the violinist and throw it in. Styx will help you.

Trust Margot. She knows our story and where we are from. She will help you in whatever way she can. She has been good to me, a trusted friend, and I consider her family.

If you don't remember me saying so before, I'm saying so now: I love you, and I miss you more than words can tell.

Your mother,
Maggie

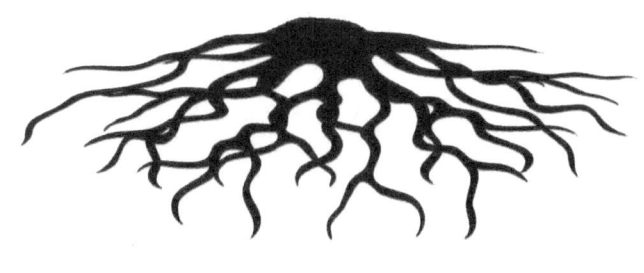

11

DOWN BY THE RIVERSIDE

NED FINALLY LIFTED HIS eyes. The brunette woman was watching him from across the table.

"You're Margot?"

"Yes. Need a hug?"

Ned gave a bark of laughter as he felt tears leak out of his eyes.

Margot was immediately there with her arms around him. Ned accepted the gesture of comfort, clutching her with one hand and the letter in the other. It took several moments for his sobs to calm and his shoulders to stop shaking as all the frustrations, disappointments, losses, and fears of the last few days hit him all at once. And in the end, he felt the better for it. Allowing himself to feel those emotions now helped him to focus his mind and concentrate on the task at hand.

"Do you know what river she's talking about?"

Margot released him and took the letter as he held it out. "I've a good idea. Come on."

She led him out the door and across the grounds outside. Gravel paths led between wooden tables arranged with cartons and pots of various types of plants, all labeled and arranged according to how much sun they required. Behind these was a garden with beautiful stone pathways, overgrown with plants and hidden under leaves, that weaved their way between flowerbeds and trees. Metal and stone statues littered the garden amidst barely flowing fountains and trellises covered in vines. It made Ned's soul hurt just to look at it.

"It needs work," Margot admitted quietly, waving her hand at the mess. "I was never much one for a green thumb. Maggie always took care o' the garden, and I took care o' the shop. I got a few people comes and helps with the nursery part, but Maggie's garden…"

Ned instantly regretted the judgment he had felt against Margot a moment earlier for not taking care of the garden properly. How painful it must be for her to have that constant reminder of someone she had lost and see it slowly dying every day.

Margot worked her way through the maze of pathways across the garden until they reached a little manmade stream that meandered through the property. A fountain bubbled nearby next to a statue of a man playing the violin. His bronze cap, filled with little coins, lay next to him on the square that made up his base. The coins were not of any currency that Ned had ever seen before, copper and stamped with an array of strange symbols.

Ned took a coin from the hat and went down to the river's edge. Ordinarily, he would have felt odd or silly, but well, odder things had been happening lately. The coin plopped into the river with a satisfying sound.

When nothing happened, Ned turned and looked at Margot. "Do you know what's supposed to happen?"

Margot shrugged.

He looked back down at the letter. Styx was supposed to help him. Well, who was Styx and where were they? "Hello?" he called out. "Styx?"

The river stirred as if moved by something within, and the figure of a woman broke through the surface. Her hair was matted and wet, while the woman herself was translucent and shimmered as if she were a hologram. Her clothes looked to be made of algae, and she wore a lilypad for a hat. In her hand, she held Ned's coin.

"I am here," she said in a voice that sounded like flowing water. "What is it that you have lost?"

"Lost?"

"You sent me a drachma. If you have lost something to the waters, I can restore it to you. What have you lost?"

"Um, an axe?"

Styx contemplated him for a moment, then sank beneath the surface. The water barely rippled, and Ned stared down at the river as he stood at the water's edge. But she had disappeared. There was nowhere she could have gone in the water that was barely a foot deep.

But a few moments later, she broke through the surface of the water again, holding a shining golden axe in her hands. It was one of the most magnificent things he had ever seen, splendid with jewels, and delicately cast, designed like a Faberge egg.

"Is this the axe that you have lost?"

As taken aback as Ned was at its beauty, as tempting as it would have been under other circumstances to take it, Ned knew that the right axe in this situation could be a matter of life and death. This was not the one he needed, nor did it match the one from his memory. "No. No, it isn't."

She disappeared again beneath the water and returned this time with an axe made of silver, similarly adorned with riches. "And what of this axe?"

Ned knew again that it was not his axe. Which he needed sooner rather than later. "Nope. Look, how many axes are down there? Or are you just playing with me? Not meaning to be rude at all, but I'm kind of in a hurry."

"Shh," Margot said. "It's a test. Don'tcha know the story?

"There's a story?"

When Styx broke through the water's surface once more, she carried a small double-bladed broadaxe. Its shaft and blades were both made of the same shiny silvery metal that glinted in the dawn's early light. "Because of your honesty, you may have your axe back. As well as the other two." She laid all three axes on the riverbank and then sank back into the water before Ned could say a word.

"Don'tcha read?" Margot asked.

"Not *that* story." Ned picked up the broadaxe and held it in his hands. It was light, so light that it would be easy to wield with one hand. *Finally.* That stupid axe that everyone was after, and that everyone wanted to kill him for. Such an ordinary looking artifact for a weapon of such power, power that so many different forces and peoples were vying for. Just to be sure, he raised the axe over his head and brought it down onto a large stone sitting by the riverbed. The stone split neatly in half without any chipping and no apparent damage to the axe.

"Thanks for your help, Margot," he said. "But I've got to run now."

"I unnerstand. Be safe. Don't forget yer other axes!"

"You keep them," Ned said, pressing them into her hands. "You get one, and I'll be back for the other."

"So ya will come back?"

"When this is all over," Ned promised. *If we're all still alive.*

He called Robin as he climbed back into the truck.

"Ned!" Robin's voice was full of concern.

"Ned, you okay?"

"I'm fine," Ned said. "How are you and Nana?"

"We're okay. Those police officers are still here. So are Mr. Kennedy and Roddy. They really want to speak with you."

Ned groaned and pressed his forehead against the rim of the steering wheel. He really wasn't in the mood to deal with the fallout of what had happened at the Kennedy house. And he had bigger things to worry about, like saving Mac. "Put them on the phone."

"Jack." Mr. Kennedy's voice sounded tired and strained.

"Please, call me Ned."

"Ned," Mr. Kennedy conceded. "Roddy has told me everything that happened. I don't deny my son Fergus' behavior, and it will be dealt with. But right now, we've both got a bigger problem. Have you found the axe yet?"

Ned hesitated to trust him. But he was going to need the help of someone like Mr. Kennedy. Someone who knew about Up Root. "Yes."

"Now what do you intend to do?"

That, Ned knew the answer to. "They beat up Nana, and they took Mac. I'm going after them."

"How do you intend to get there?"

"The beanstalk."

"And do you know where to find it?"

Ned rubbed at his tired face. "No," he admitted.

"I do. You know the trailhead parking lot for the Zebra and Sandy Trails off of 1375?"

"Yes."

"Then I'll meet you there."

As he turned the key in the ignition, Ned knew he was going to need more than an axe if he was going into enemy territory. More immediately, he was going to need food and coffee before he passed out. There was a Buc-ee's on the way back to the interstate, so he stopped for gas, a southwest style chicken wrap, and the largest coffee they offered.

He stopped at Nana's before heading further north to the trailheads. Going into Nana's closet, he dragged out the wooden chest. He rummaged through the collection inside, selecting the weapons he figured would be handiest to have. The knives and crossbows got stuffed into his backpack. He strapped on the double gun shoulder holster and loaded the revolvers.

It was time to go hunt a giant.

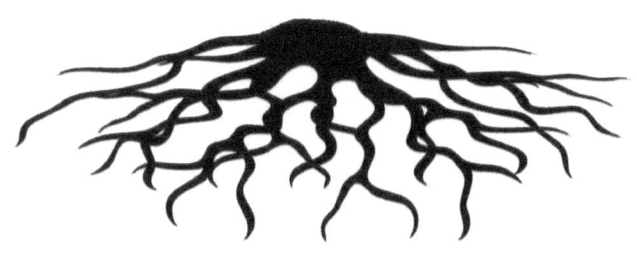

12

UP THE ROOTS

RODDY AND MR. KENNEDY were already waiting for Ned at the trailhead as he pulled up in Nana's truck. A part of him still hesitated to trust Mr. Kennedy. How did he know that they weren't there to jump him and take the axe?

He stepped out of the truck, keeping his distance, ready to draw one of the revolvers with his bandaged left arm and holding his motorcycle helmet with his good arm.

Mr. Kennedy raised his eyebrows slightly as he surveyed Ned's collection of weapons, his eyes coming to rest on the axe tucked through his belt. "Glad to see you have not come empty handed. Good thought on the helmet."

"Yeah, really came in handy during my last fight." Ned watched him warily.

Mr. Kennedy sighed. "Let's hope it works as well on ogres and giants," he said, turning towards the woods.

Then he just sort of melted towards the ground, sinking downwards and then forwards, and then there was a wolf standing on all fours where Mr. Kennedy had been. Ned hadn't actually seen one of the Kennedys change into wolf form before. As much as he had thought he really shouldn't be surprised by anything anymore, it was still unnerving to watch. Like his sons, Mr. Kennedy's wolf form was white with tinges of brown across the fur. Roddy's fur, as he shifted in the same manner, was much thicker and nearly all white.

Mr. Kennedy started leading them down one of the trails but then turned off of it into the woods. The mud was still thick, but the sun was out, making it easier to see as they wove through the thick undergrowth. Not that Ned didn't feel any less lost. Even with their footprints being left in the squelching layer of river silt, it still would have been very difficult to find his way back.

The wolves were both covered with mud

by the time they arrived. The giant green beanstalk rose out of the earth amongst the pine trees and bracken. It was a good four feet in diameter, made of three enormous green stalks twisted together. At the intersection of these three, right where they came out of the ground, was a gap leading down into the roots.

Ned felt the anger and frustration rising again and swallowed hard. That stupid plant that had turned his world upside down. And on his belt was the cause of it all. Some stupid magical axe that for some reason everybody wanted and was going to lead to the end of the world.

Beside him, Mr. Kennedy and Roddy morphed back into human form.

"You'll need these." Mr. Kennedy handed out a couple of headlamps. "I hope you're not claustrophobic," he added, stepping forward into the midst of the three stalks and lowering himself down into the gap.

Ned opened his mouth, then shut it and shook his head. No, it might be bothering him, but it should really wait for a better time. He really should be focusing on finding Mac and the imminent danger for all of them, but he just had to know.

"Sorry," he stopped Roddy as the younger

Kennedy stepped toward the beanstalk. "Not trying to be rude, but question about the whole wolf thing."

"It's the clothes isn't it," Roddy said, eyes twinkling a little.

"How does that work, exactly?"

"Today, we have them specially made and 'customized'… enchanted, if you want to put it that way. They automatically disappear and reappear as we change in and out of wolf form. Before that, I'm certain it made for some very awkward situations."

Ned nodded as Roddy lowered himself down after his uncle. That would certainly be handy, as it allowed them to change back and forth at will without worrying about where their clothes were going to be. It had also kept their clothes from getting torn or muddied as they trekked through the woods, he noted as he looked down at his own ripped clothing and mud-soaked jeans. He wondered how much the transition from wolf to human form had affected Fergus's injuries after the fight. Did they have different impacts in human versus wolf form?

He shook off the questions and turned his attention back to the beanstalk. There would be plenty of opportunity to ask about all that later –

if he survived all this.

After putting on his helmet and strapping the headlamp to it, he followed Roddy and slid down between the stalks. The gap in the roots smelled of green plants and must and earth. Between the mud on his shoes, the smooth texture of the stalks, and the weakness of his injured left arm, it was quite slippery, and he tried not to slide down onto Roddy's head. Somewhere along the way, Ned realized that the roots were now horizontal, and that they were edging along the narrow gap between damp strands of roots that dusted them with dirt as they brushed past.

"Do you remember the world on the other side?" Mr. Kennedy asked, dragging himself sideways along a narrow section.

Ned shook his head. "Nope."

"What was your plan then?"

"Find Mac. Kill the giant."

Mr. Kennedy stopped and turned to look back at Ned, tilting his headlamp up so that he didn't blind Ned and Roddy. "You may have plenty of weapons in that backpack, but you are only one man. You also have the axe, which makes you a target. The giant will be looking for you, just as much as you are looking for him. There was a reason the ogres took Mackenzie. They knew that you would follow."

Ned mulled these thoughts over as he stared at the brown tangle of roots in front of him. This was all true, but it wasn't like he knew of anyone in Up Root to get in contact with. He didn't know what it looked like. He didn't know anyone else to ask for help. But it was the only way he knew to get Mac back.

"The citizens of Up Root – they are eager to be rid of Thumbling and his tyranny. Even some of the giants in Up Root are willing to help us."

Ned looked back up at Mr. Kennedy, who flinched in the direct light of Ned's headlamp. Ned moved it quickly. "Hang on, how do you know that?"

"Because while Nana has been helping you search for the axe, I was looking for the beanstalk. Getting in touch with someone on the other side unnoticed was the difficult part. Thumbling picked a very secure location to plant his beanstalk, in the grounds of the old castle in a walled courtyard so as to control access to it. He has ogres and giants posted to guard it. But I was able to get a message through. Like I said, many of the giants are worried. Now that access to the giant world has also been restored, they fear that he will take over it as he did Up Root. We have been working together, but Thumbling's attack on Nana moved our timeline forward. Time we still needed to prepare. Let us hope that what we have done already will be able to suffice."

"What *were* you able to do?" Roddy asked.

"I called in a favor," Mr. Kennedy said. "There happens to be a very prominent gang member I defended in court. I was able to secure a sizeable stash of firearms from his gunrunner."

Ned shook his head. Never did he think he would hear that Mr. Kennedy was being helped by gang members smuggling illegal weapons. But then again, he himself had traded a favor with a dangerous witch. A deal he didn't yet know all the repercussions of. "And these firearms are where now?"

"Smuggled into Up Root during the night by the rats, and hopefully, distributed to the correct parties. But we'll find out when we get there." Mr. Kennedy adjusted his headlamp and moved to continue along the roots.

"I'm sorry, rats?"

"We don't have much time. Is that really the question you want to ask right now?" Mr. Kennedy gave him a pained look.

Ned closed his eyes and shook his head again. Of course, it wasn't. "So, do you know where to find Mac?"

"Probably in the tower with the princess. It should be in the same castle grounds as the beanstalk."

About an hour later, Ned finally caught a glimpse of light ahead. The beanstalk was now climbing up again, and Ned struggled to make it with one arm. Slight tremors shook the ground in rhythms. Loud deep voices echoed their way down to the three climbers.

Mr. Kennedy stopped, forcing Roddy and Ned to do so as well. "When you come up, do so carefully to make sure you aren't seen. There will be a gate on one side of the courtyard with bars just far enough apart to squeeze through. We'll meet on the other side."

Mr. Kennedy was speaking quietly so that his voice would not carry to the surface, so Roddy passed the message down to Ned. Ned couldn't see what all he was doing because Roddy was blocking his view, but a few moments later, they were moving upward again. Mr. Kennedy and Roddy were no longer above him. And then Ned's head rose through the earth. Looking around, he didn't see either of them.

The beanstalk grew in the middle of a round courtyard, surrounded by a wall of gray stone blocks, worn with age and chipped in a few places. Two iron gates stood at opposite ends. The thumping they had heard down below was made by two ogres whose footsteps would create tremors in the ground below.

Only the ogres were no longer standing. They lay prone on the ground against the wall of the courtyard by one of the gates. Just how had Mr. Kennedy managed that? The other gate had a few rods missing, creating a gap just wide enough for a body to fit through. Ned pulled himself out of the gap in the beanstalk and slipped across the few feet of stone tiles covered in moss and vines. As he slid through the gate, a hand grabbed him and pulled him to one side behind the wall. Mr. Kennedy held a finger to his lips, signaling Ned to be quiet, then patted his shoulder and pointed ahead.

A stone pathway led them across the overgrown grounds to another stone wall, not far away. They slid through what used to be a wooden door, now rotted and half gone, and found themselves beside a street. Ned stopped short as he saw what lay on the other side of it.

Mr. Kennedy tugged on his arm,

redirecting his attention as they turned right to follow the street. Ned couldn't help but look left as they kept walking. The city looked like something out of a post-apocalyptic movie mixed with Greek ruins. It reminded him of pictures of Europe after World War 2. Half of the buildings lay in ruin, while the other half reflected the poverty and struggles of those who still lived within. A world torn apart by war and never fully rebuilt.

People moved quietly and quickly through the streets under the sunlight struggling to shine through the layer of clouds overhead. By the way they sneaked glances across the street, Ned had a feeling that he and the Kennedys did not blend in as well as he would have liked. But the people didn't seem to let it slow their pace, continuing on their way without any hesitation. There were no ogres walking the streets that he could see.

Ned turned his attention back to the gray stone wall on his right. The street and the wall ran parallel to each other, stretching in a straight line behind and ahead of them. Mr. Kennedy was sticking as close to the wall as possible, as if to avoid being seen by anyone looking over it.

"Cross." Without slowing his stride, Mr. Kennedy stepped off the curb and onto the street.

Ned and Roddy turned and followed him.

On the other side, Mr. Kennedy led them away from the main street and then turned right. Following a side street, they walked parallel to the main street. From there, they could see more of the castle grounds and observe it from a safe distance.

Mr. Kennedy didn't appear to be as interested in the castle itself, casting a constant watchful eye around them, much like the people of Up Root. Ned's eyes were drawn to the tall towers that he could see over the top of the wall. Not that he knew what to look for.

"Ned," Roddy said from behind him.

Ned turned. Roddy had stopped a few feet behind them and was staring intently across the street. Walking back towards him, Ned looked to see what Roddy was pointing at.

And there she was. His very own Mac. His blood boiled as he watched her being carried by a giant. The giant held her in his fist as he walked across a field and up a staircase to the battlements on the far side of the field. She was, as expected, squirming and hitting and kicking. Probably shouting insults, if Ned knew her. The giant looked out of place in a castle built for humans, like an adult walking through a miniature village built for six year olds. Now he was walking along a bridge from the battlements to a tower in the middle of the field. He leaned over and lifted the roof as if it were the lid of a jewelry box, dropping Mac inside.

13

THE GIANT, THE PRINCESS, AND THE TOWER

NED MOVED TO STEP forward.

Roddy grabbed the back of his jacket. "Wait."

After lowering the roof back onto the tower, the giant walked away, wringing his hand as he did so. Mac's resistance must have hurt him a little.

"I'm going after her," Ned said.

"Remember, it may be a trap," Mr. Kennedy warned. "Go ahead, but be careful."

"What about you?" Roddy asked his uncle.

"I'm going to check on your backup." Mr. Kennedy gave his nephew's shoulder a slight squeeze and continued down the street.

Ned turned down an alley and headed back towards the main street, Roddy right behind him. After crossing the road, they walked along the wall, looking for a way through it. There was a gap where part of the wall had caved in, and they climbed through to the other side.

The open grassy area in front of them was about the size of a football field, with the tower in the middle of it. They would be completely exposed with no cover and nothing to hide behind, but the coast appeared to be clear.

Ned looked at Roddy. "What do you think?"

"I think you're going to owe me a few favors," Roddy said. "Looks clear though."

Ned shook his head and gave a half smile.

The two of them ran across the field to the base of the stone tower. Ned wished he had a way to let Mac know that he was there. The window at the top of the tower was too high up to call out without drawing attention. There was no way into the tower from down below, no doors or stairs. And the bridge that the giant had walked across was missing a section, leaving a gap between the bridge and the tower. The rest of it was still supported by stone arches like an aqueduct. The giant must have had long enough arms to reach across the gap.

"Jaaaaaaccck!" a thunderous voice rang across the field and echoed off of the stones around them.

And then from the walls and buildings surrounding the field, ogres burst out of the shadows and moved in on them. Roddy and Ned were surrounded, with nowhere to run, as the monsters charged at them from all directions. Beside him, Roddy morphed into wolf form as Ned drew one of his pistols. He was grateful that Nana had kept the double action revolvers in such good condition. And for that handgun course she had insisted they all take together last summer.

"Ned!" Mac shouted above him.

Ned looked up briefly to see Mac's face pressed through the bars of the window, high up in the tower. "Little busy, dear," he called up, turning his attention back to the charging ogres.

His first shot went wide, ricocheting off of the stone wall in the distance. There were so many of them, he almost didn't know where to start. He breathed out to steady himself, gripped the gun with both hands, and fired again. Four more shots rang out. Three ogres fell, one after another. Ned pulled his other revolver and fired as many shots as he could before the ogres closed in.

Dropping the guns, he pulled the axe out of his belt in time to duck and swing. Beside him, Roddy was snapping, growling, twisting, and biting. He moved too quickly for the ogres to get a hold of. Ned was glad he was wearing his helmet. A few blows from the ogres' clubs bounced off the helmet, without doing him any serious damage. Wielding the axe was surprisingly easy and natural. It required very little strength to swing it around and slice through his enemies. And with such big targets, accuracy wasn't an issue.

And then there were none. Ned swung around to face the next enemy, but all that remained of the ogres were bodies already turning into mud. Except for the ones just arriving on the field.

"Run!" Roddy growled.

The two of them ran for the cover of a few stone structures off to one side of the field. They entered into what had once been the Great Hall of the castle. Two rows of enormous stone pillars rose to meet an arched ceiling three stories high. The cloudy sunlight filtered through the dusty floor-to-ceiling windows. Roddy and Ned glanced about for a moment, then ran for the cover of the closest pillar.

"Jack!"

The deep, gravelly voice echoed through the hall, rumbled through the ground, curdled Ned's blood, and froze him in his tracks.

"I was hoping you would return, boy," the voice rumbled from the far end of the hall. "You have something that I want." Heavy footsteps punctuated the words. And they were coming towards him.

Ned glanced over at Roddy. The wolf's head was down, hair standing up on end, and eyes staring into the darkness, searching for the owner of the voice.

The footsteps were coming closer.

"Your little girlfriend has been waiting for you," Thumbling continued. "Knew you'd come for her. Where's my axe, Jack?"

Ned gritted his teeth. If someone called him 'Jack' one more time…

The footsteps stopped right beside his pillar, and a giant foot settled into view right next to him. "I'll find you eventually, Jack. Come out, come out, wherever you are."

Ned let all his frustrations out in one blow. "My name is Ned," he shouted, raising the axe above his head and swinging down. An ordinary axe would have glanced off the thick leather shoe. This one went straight through shoe, flesh, and bone.

"Run!" Ned shouted, turning back towards the way they had come.

A deep thunderous roar shook the walls, so deep and loud it shattered the glass windows.

But above the scream of pain and the breaking of glass rose another sound. Gunfire and explosions boomed and echoed off of stone and earth across the city. Mr. Kennedy's militia had arrived.

"He's here! Ned – Jack's here," Mac said, turning to the other prisoner in the tower.

"I hope he's brought the axe." The woman was about ten years older than Mac, just reaching her thirties.

"Time to go, your highness." Mac rubbed her hands together.

"Go?! And how would you suggest we do

that?"

Mac rolled her eyes. The Princess Navia did seem to have a pessimistic spirit – not that she could blame her.

The woman had been locked inside the tower by Thumbling for the last eight years. He would take her out occasionally, usually at dinner time. He had kept her alive as a way to help control the people of Up Root. The tower itself had two different levels, a fully functional bathroom, books, and the convenience of electricity and running water. Honestly, not a bad place if you were going to be imprisoned. But any cage can destroy the soul and spirit, no matter how gilded.

"Haven't you ever heard of Rapunzel?" Mac pulled her pocket knife out of her jeans. Thankfully, the ogres hadn't even thought about taking it out of her pocket. "Time for a haircut. I believe you're about ten years overdue for one anyways."

Ned led Thumbling on a game of hide and seek. Once outside the Great Hall, he flattened himself up against the building, waiting for the giant to come barging through. As Thumbling came crashing after him, Ned raised his axe again and brought it down onto the giant's other foot.

He darted away as the giant screamed once more. Up a flight of stairs to his left. He may not have had as much strength, but Ned had the advantage of unhampered speed. The giant hobbled after him, slowed greatly now that both feet were injured.

In the field below and across the streets and castle grounds, guns blazed, and ogres roared. People and wolves fought ogres and giants. Giants were fighting giants and ogres. There were quite a few other creatures as well, some even coming from the ground beneath the beanstalk.

Ned stumbled to a stop as a block of stone the size of a washing machine landed on the stairs in front of him, and rolled towards him. Trapped between stone and giant, Ned avoided both by jumping. Off the staircase and down to the ground. He tried rolling to break his fall, but the impact of jumping from that height still nearly knocked the wind out of him. Jolts of pain traveled from his feet up into his thighs, and his bandaged arm was tingling and throbbing.

He staggered to his feet, forcing himself to keep moving. Thumbling was coming after him, sword in hand. The four-foot longsword looked like little more than a dagger in the giant's hand, but that didn't make it any less dangerous. The giant almost didn't need the enchantment of the sword to break down walls. And if it were to even touch Ned, there would be no chance of survival.

Ned ran towards the battlements, seeking cover under the bridge and dodging around the pillars for cover. But with a swing of Thumbling's sword, one of the pillars met its end and crumbled to the ground. Ned ducked as chunks of stone tumbled about him, reeling as several of them glanced off his helmet. At this rate, the entire castle would end up on the ground.

He wove back and forth amongst the pillars, working his way back towards the battlements. His feet were still hurting, and the impact of each step sent another jolt up his legs. His left arm was useless and hurting. But he was still faster than the injured giant.

At the far end of the battlements, Ned dashed up the stairs. They slowed Ned down a little, but he had enough of a lead that he could still stay ahead of the injured Thumbling. Ned reached the top and ran along the battlements. But now there were some ogres coming from the other end of the wall. Once again, he was trapped, caught between stampeding ogres and an angry giant.

There was nowhere to go but the bridge. He raced along it, staggering to a stop as he reached the other end. Here the section that connected the bridge to the tower was missing, and he stood on the edge of a fifty-foot drop. Jumping wasn't going to work this time.

"Ned!"

Ned looked up, and there was Mac. His own dear, sweet Mac, only ten feet away from him. So close, and yet too far.

"Ned, catch!" Mac tossed something towards him out the window.

Ned caught the end of the braided rope, fumbling with it for a moment. He glanced over his shoulder. Thumbling was only steps behind him. Without thinking any further, Ned jumped. Thumbling made a last effort to leap forward and grab at him but was too late.

Ned swung down and forward towards the tower, then past it in a large arc, up and up. He was on the return swing now. In a split second, his mind took in the scene, the giant on the end of the bridge, the ogres coming up behind it. And the two remaining pillars beneath the bridge. Gripping the rope in his right hand, he shifted the axe to his left. As he neared the edge of the bridge again, Ned reached out and down, swinging at the pillar beneath Thumbling.

The roar of collapsing stone and falling giant rumbled through the air and shook the ground as the bridge collapsed, taking Thumbling and ogres with it. And then there was just a pile of rubble on the field and the last remaining pillar sticking out of it.

The fallen giant gathered his arms and legs beneath him with great effort. But before he could rise again, another giant strode through the midst of the battle that had ceased in realization of what had happened. Picking up Thumbling's sword, the giant raised it high above his head with both hands and drove it through Thumbling's heart.

Ned wanted to look away, but his eyes were glued to this second giant. This giant who now possessed the magical sword. Was he going to take it for himself and come after Ned? But the giant tossed the sword aside and spat upon the fallen enemy in disgust.

Ned closed his eyes in relief and buried his face against the rope.

"Nice shot!" Mac called from above.

Ned looked up. He was so relieved and numb and pumped up with adrenaline and ready to collapse at the same time, he could only think of one thing to say. "Is this hair?"

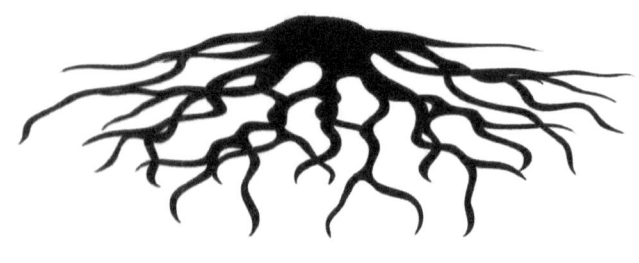

14

RETURN TO NORMALCY

"SO, YOU ARE JACK."

Ned somehow didn't feel like correcting a princess who had been imprisoned for the last eight years. The woman, who was about ten years older than him, regarded him for a moment and then turned and surveyed the field around them. The Princess Navia was tall and willowy, her black hair that had been cut to make Mac's rope waving around her head like a halo. Her gaze as she surveyed the ruins of her father's kingdom was cold and calculating.

Ned also turned to look around them at this place that was so foreign and yet vaguely familiar.

Once it was clear that they featured in the minority, the ogres had fled, disappearing through the city and out into the wilderness beyond. The giant that had killed Thumbling helped Ned down to the ground before he could slip and fall. It took longer to help Mac and the Princess Nivia down from the tower. With the bridge collapsed, there was no way to reach the door or the roof, and it had taken the friendly giants a little bit of time to construct a pile of stones that was tall enough and sturdy enough to climb on.

Ned took off his helmet and waited as they worked on it, conscious of the sideways glances the people were giving him and the quiet whispering as they milled about the castle grounds, scavenging and cleaning after the battle. But he kept his eyes on the work around the tower and the face waiting for him at the top.

"You alright?" Roddy approached him, back in human form. "Here."

"Oh, yes, thank you," Ned said, taking the pistols that Roddy had retrieved for him. "Nana probably wouldn't forgive me if I didn't bring them back." He snapped them into their holsters.

"Are you alright?"

"I'm fine." Roddy folded his arms and stood beside Ned, watching the construction of a pile of stones large enough to reach the top of the tower. "How's the arm?"

"Hurts."

"You should probably get that checked out again when you get back to the hospital."

"I'm not going to turn into a werewolf, am I?"

Roddy's mouth twitched at the corners. "Probably not."

"Good. I don't want to have to get all my clothes altered."

And then, the temporary staircase was ready, and the giant that had helped Ned down from the rope was able to get to the top.

So now Ned stood in front of an actual princess while waiting for Mac to be brought down.

Mr. Kennedy was the first to greet the princess, offering her father's longsword to her. She had greeted him by name and now stood gripping its hilt with one hand, resting the point on the ground while she surveyed her people and city.

Ned wondered at the exchange. Nana had

said that the Kennedys were old Up Root blood. Just how connected was the family that the princess knew him by name after all these years?

And then, there was Mac safe and sound on the ground. She immediately came up, grabbed him, and kissed him. Ned held her tight. The scent of her cherry blossom perfume and the taste of her sweet lips. The way her hair curved round her face. The sparkle in her eyes. His Mac.

"Nana?" Mac asked.

"She's okay," Ned assured her. "She's in the hospital, but she's okay."

"Good. Last I saw of her, she was clubbing at an ogre with the butt of her shotgun. And Robin? Is she safe?"

"Yep, she's okay too. She's with Nana."

"Good." Mac hugged him once more.

"What about you?" Ned asked into the top of her brown hair.

"I've got the most badass boyfriend in the universe, and I get to say that this was the most exciting spring break on record."

Ned laughed. If she could still have that impossible optimism that he loved so much about her, then she was going to be fine.

"Will you be returning to Up Root to stay, Jack?" the Princess Nivia asked, turning back towards him.

Ned hesitated for a few moments. It was something he hadn't even considered. He may have been born in Up Root, but he had no memory of it, no ties to it anymore. "No, ma'am," he said finally. A part of him wondered belatedly if that was the appropriate way to address a princess. "No, this may be where I came from, but I have a whole life in Down Root. That's… that's where my home is now."

The princess nodded in understanding.

Ned looked down, remembering the axe that he had stuck into the ground beside himself. It would be a relief to be rid of it. Keeping it from Thumbling was one thing, but if anyone could have a claim on the axe, it was probably the princess. "Here," Ned said, offering the axe towards the princess. "You should have this."

The princess shook her head. "No, I will take my father's sword, but I am thinking it is best that the two are not kept in the same place. You have kept it well all these years. So the safekeeping of the axe, I entrust to you. It is your official responsibility now."

Ned winced deep inside and pursed his lips. Why him? It was a responsibility he would gladly have passed on. As far as the axe was concerned, it was a whole world of trouble, and if it really was an end-of-the-world kind of scenario, why on earth would they want to pick him?

"Do you have a good place for safekeeping the axe?"

Ned was about to protest and insist he didn't have any way to keep it safe. But then, he was reminded of his mother's solution. Probably the most secure person and place to entrust it to. "Actually, yes, I think I know a place."

"Very good," the princess nodded.

Ned followed her gaze out over the city of Up Root. "And, what about you?" he asked. "What about Up Root?"

"Up Root will rebuild," she said firmly. "And I will take my father's throne. There is much work to be done here."

Ned nodded. He hoped that the princess and the people of Up Root would be able to now that Thumbling was gone. "Well, we should probably be going. We have people who are very worried about us."

"Good," Princess Nivia said. "It must be nice to have someone to worry about you. Thank you, Jack. And you also, Mackenzie. You two take care of each other." She turned and began to walk towards Mr. Kennedy.

Ned took Mac's hand and squeezed it. It was time to go home.

"Oh, and Jack."

Ned turned. Nivia had stopped and was looking over her shoulder at them.

"Don't disappear again. I may be needing to call upon you in the future." She continued towards Mr. Kennedy.

Ned didn't know how to feel about that. "You coming with?" he asked Roddy.

Roddy nodded. *"Someone's* got to make sure you get back to your truck safely."

Back down the beanstalk it was. The three of them worked their way through the root system. The darkness of the tunnel finally ended, and Ned popped his head through the opening to see the bright sunny rays of mid-afternoon. He used both arms to pull himself out of the hole. Then he turned to help Mac and Roddy out.

"So, what next?" Mac asked.

"I'm up for anything so long as it does not involve dragons," Ned took her hand again. So long as he had Mac.

"This way back to the truck." Roddy led the way through the woods.

"I wonder if those policemen are still there or not."

The policemen *were* still there, not that they were very happy about it. Dawson was napping uncomfortably in one corner, while Briggs sat in a chair by the door, holding his chin in his right, resting his elbow on his knee, and drumming with his left hand on his other.

"Well, *finally!*" Nana was the one who saw them at the door first. "Where have you been?!"

Briggs looked up at them and glowered.

"Thank you so much," Ned said as Robin and Mac crowded around Nana's bed. "We really – "

"Coffee," Briggs interrupted, rising heavily from his seat.

"Sorry, sir?"

"The only thing I need from you is a cup of coffee. I don't want to know where you've been or what you've been doing. I don't even need your thanks, because I won't be saying 'you're welcome'. Just give me coffee."

Ned made a quick getaway downstairs where he bought two of the largest, most caffeinated options that the fake Starbucks had to offer and then returned to give them to the police officers as a peace offering.

Briggs took a long draught of the steaming hot beverage and breathed a heavy sigh. "Right. We're going."

"Just tell me," Dawson stopped in the doorway, "did you figure a way to fix whatever problem was happening, or can we expect to see you... again..."

"Over for now," Ned assured him. "I don't think you'll be seeing us anytime soon."

"Oh, good." Dawson darted out quickly as if he was worried Ned would change his mind.

Nana was none too happy when Ned and Mac told her about meeting Babba Ygga. As harmless as three little leaves might seem, she warned, these things had a way of coming back to haunt you. But there was not much to do about it since the deal had already been made. And the witch would certainly hold him to his end of the deal.

Margot was thrilled that Ned planned on coming out to help at the nursery more often. Half the shop was legally his now anyways, and the garden did so need someone to take care of it. It would also provide a home base for Ned's gardening business to run out of.

Ned didn't tell anyone about taking the axe back to The Enchanted Garden, not even Margot. What she didn't know would hopefully keep her from being in any danger. The axe was safe enough with Styx.

As for Fergus, Roddy informed Ned that Mr. Kennedy had taken him and handed him over to the Princess Nivia. Werewolf problems were best dealt with in Up Root fashion. Princess Nivia had sentenced him to being a convict laborer, helping to rebuild Up Root.

So far, the princess hadn't called upon Ned to help with anything else. He hoped it stayed that way. He was ready to go back to as normal a life as he could, where the biggest problem in life was business calculus and not ogres.

But before they headed back to the university, Nana insisted they have a celebration dinner.

The brass and crystal chandelier shone down on the cheerful party of people gathered at the dining room table. From the way the party went on, one would never have guessed that the house had been broken into just a few days before, or that almost everyone there had faced certain death in the last few days.

But they were eating off of Nana's fine silver and turquoise patterned China, what hadn't been smashed by ogres anyways, and making do with some of the broken bits, and laughing all the while. One of the armrests on one of the chairs had been glued and duct taped in place. Other than that, and a few gouges in the woodwork that Nana, Robin, Ned, and Mac had just not been able to get out, almost everything was back into place.

Margot had come as a particular honored guest, and everyone was delighted to meet her. Roddy made a brief appearance. Nana had even sent invitations to their two new favorite policemen, but not surprisingly, they had both declined.

It had been a while since the formal dining room had seen such a party. Blue and magnolia print wallpaper with polished wood trim covered the walls. The long cherry wood table matched the fancy China cabinets along the walls. Dried flower bouquets filled enormous vases in each of the corners. At the head of the table, hung on the wall for decoration, was The List, the Annual Spring Break Bucket List that this year would not be completed. Next to it was a new list labelled "Things We Survived":

Attack by Fergus

Outside, an old crone watched the cheerful lights in the house from the forest's edge. Resting both hands on her walking stick, she shifted her gaze to the gathering storm clouds.

A wolf came trotting up beside her and changed into the form of a man. "What have you done, old woman?" Mr. Kennedy grunted.

"I have done what I have done, and is my own business," Babba Ygga said evenly.

"Your business has a habit of affecting all of us."

"I not hear you complain before. Especially

when it was to your benefit."

Unable to argue with that, Mr. Kennedy sighed in disgust and turned to leave.

"Our deal still stands, Kennedy," the witch warned without taking her eyes off of the house ahead. "See that you not forget."

Mr. Kennedy grimaced before turning back into a wolf and trotting away.

The old woman stayed and watched the party for a moment longer, then disappeared into the woods. And the rain started the fall.

If you enjoyed Down Root

Three children embark on a quest to save their father – to the edge of the world and beyond.

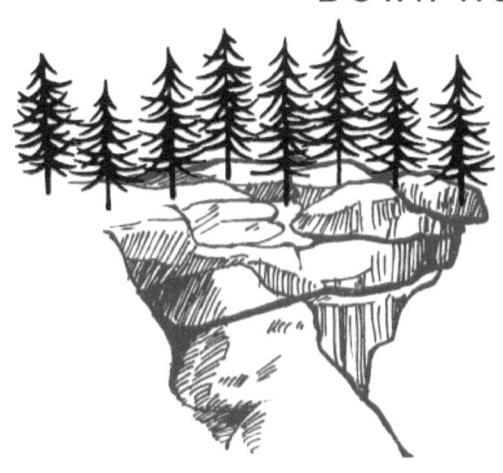

1
When the Children Are Sent Away

THE GIRLS SAID AFTERWARD that it was Walter's fault. He had started the day off in a bad mood, which worsened when the rains came because it meant that he could not go outside and train. His main goal at this point in his life was to be made a squire. And how was he supposed to become a squire if the stupid rain kept him from training?

"Oh, stop complaining, Walter," Airdella said, eyes rolling. "For pity's sake!"

"I wasn't complaining!"

"You were sulking, then."

"Was not."

"Was too."

Conscience kept Walter from continuing the argument. Instead, he chose to glare at her and turn sullenly away. Pressing his nose against the glass, he stared down at the courtyard below in which he would have been training right then, had it not been for the rain. The usually dusty earth of the corrals and arena was quickly turning into an impossible muddy mess. He turned when he felt a tug on his sleeve, and his face softened a little. He had a soft spot for his younger sister Amaryllis, who was his favorite.

"What do you want?"

Amaryllis simply looked up at him with her odd blue eyes. Though she was eleven years old, she had become very quiet since their mother had died, rarely speaking to people she did not know. Holding up the box that held their heavy stone chess pieces, she motioned toward the chess table.

"Not right now, Amy."

"Why not, Walt?" Airdella broke in. "It's a form of fighting after all and will distract you."

"I don't feel like it."

"Well, play anyways."

"Are you ordering me to play?"

"Yes, Walter, I am."

"You can't make me!"

"Oh, yes, I can! I'm sixteen years old, and you're more than a year younger than I am!"

"Well, you still can't! I'm not going to!"

"Yes, you are!"

Walter lost control, grabbed one of the chess pieces from the box, and threw it at Airdella. He missed, and it landed on the tray holding their porcelain tea things, sending them all to the floor where they shattered into dozens of tiny pieces.

"Now, look what you've done!" Airdella shouted, shaking tea and bits of porcelain from her dress.

"Good riddance," Walter muttered. He hated tea.

She leapt up and slapped Walter. That was

only the beginning of many punches to follow.

Amy, as Amaryllis was called by her family, scurried back. She had seen enough of their fights to know not to get close or interfere; she began to pick up the broken teacups instead. Gently she picked up the broken chess piece from the wreckage. It had been the black knight, and the horse's eyes were made of tiny rubies. She squeezed it in her hand and closed her eyes tightly as the fighting continued.

An exclamation of "Oh my goodness gracious!" made the fighters freeze, fists in midair. Amy's nurse and Airdella's governess both stood in the doorway, their mouths agape in astonishment. I need not describe the lecture they got before being sent to bed without any supper. Airdella had a big black eye that was starting to turn purple, and Walter's cheek was puffy and swollen. Amy's hands were cut from handling the broken porcelain, so her nurse took her upstairs and washed and bandaged her hands before having her supper sent up to her.

The next morning, all three of them woke

to find their traveling trunks being packed. In response to all their questions, the only answer they got was that they were being sent away. When asked where to, the answer was "out in the country somewhere." When asked for how long, the maids only responded that they didn't know, that it all depended. What it was dependent on, no one would tell them.

And so, the children went to the one person who they knew would be behind all of this and might or might not be willing to tell them. Their father, King Conrad, stood by the gate of the castle talking in hushed tones to his good friend and trusted knight Sir Roderick. It was hard to read beyond his usual worried and vague expression, one that he had taken on and carried for years since the death of their mother, the Queen. His retreat into a reserved aloofness had created some distance between him and his children, a chasm they never seemed to be able to reach across anymore. But they could still see it in his eyes, hard as he might try to mask the rest of his face – the pain, the same pain they all felt deep inside. He greeted and spoke with them in brief and reserved tones, seeming not to hear or acknowledge their questions. A short while later, he had hugged them, and they were then packed into a carriage and hurried off.

Amy sat next to Airdella, white-faced and sobbing a little as she struggled to hold back her tears. Walter sat across from them, his brow furrowed much like his father's into lines of worry. He did not say anything, but he was picturing very vividly the scene in the nursery the night before. But if they were being sent away as a punishment for bad behavior, then why would Amy be coming as well?

Airdella was probably thinking the same thing, but she never spoke of it afterward, so we do not know for sure. Her face had drawn into its inscrutable mask of tight lips and hardened eyes, a mask she had learned to wear over years of court politics and expectations. "They didn't tell you anything either, did they, Walt?" she asked.

"No." He sighed. "We must have done something awful to get sent away and not be told what's happening."

They stopped at an inn for the night, and early the next morning, before the sun was fully up, they started off again. They were all too tired to care when they first got into the carriage, but an hour later, they had turned off the main road and onto a country road, and every rock and hole announced its presence with a jarring jolt. By the second night, they were all too glad to leave the carriage to sleep in the rough country inn. They were off before dawn the next morning, rattling down even more remote country roads. The landscape changed from gently rolling slopes of sweet thick grass and pine trees to more pronounced and rocky hills of course grasses dotted with pecan and mesquite trees.

It was midafternoon on the fifth day when they arrived at a large stone wall covered with grape vines which continued as far as they could see in both directions. A strong gate was the only thing that interrupted the greenish gray mass, except for a vine-covered turret to the left of the gate.

Walter stepped out of the carriage, glad to

be free of it and its merciless jostling, and breathed in the scent of clover and roses. Lots of them. "Where are we?" he asked, turning to the coachman.

"Dorrian's Cottage," he answered, pausing for a moment from helping the footman remove their trunks. "Sir Dorrian is a retired knight, Your Majesties."

The gate swung inward a small way, complaining loudly on its hinges, and an old man came out. The first thing they noted about him was his height. He was the kind of person that is easy to spot in a crowd. And though he was obviously old, he was neither wrinkled nor weak looking. When he spoke, it was in a surprisingly soft voice. "Well! Welcome to my cottage, Your Majesties!"

He did not sound as surprised as they felt.

"My Lord Dorrian," the coachman said, bowing low.

"Enough! No need for the whole bowing business, my good man."

"No, sir." The coachman quickly straightened, looking a little awkward. "His Majesty, the King Conrad, commanded that I give this to you." He held out a letter sealed with the King's signet.

"Yes, thank you. Now that the ceremonies are over, you must all come in and have some tea." He turned and pushed both the gates wide open.

They were greeted again by the strong scent of clover and roses. Inside the walls lay a vast expanse of grassy fields, stands of trees, and a small pool. A stone house stood a small way from the gate. It was a long, two-story building, covered with vines and morning glories and roses. A chimney smoked at each end, and a fountain splashed on the stone patio.

Amy raced up to the fountain and held her hand beneath the sparkling droplets that tumbled down.

"Do you like them?" Sir Dorrian asked.

She nodded in reply.

"It's so beautiful here." Airdella sighed. "It reminds me of the East Wing back home."

A pang of sadness hit them all as they suddenly realized how much they missed home. They had never been more than three miles away from the castle grounds in their entire life, and now, they found themselves five days from home, with no notion of where they were or why they were there. Walter was the only one, however, who caught the worried glances that the coachman, footman, and knight exchanged.

The tea was refreshing to all except Walter. He was a little intimidated by the knight, and so he had no intention of asking for something besides tea. He forced down one cup and stuck to the blueberry muffins.

The coach left soon afterward, and then Dorrian showed them to their rooms. The girls had rooms across the hall from each other at the east end of the second story, and Walter had a room of his own at the west end. The rooms were simply furnished with old but solid oak bedsteads, plain white coverlets, and carved cedar wardrobes to keep their clothes in. Plain as it was, it was refreshing and clean feeling, instead of the cluttered stuffy rooms at the castle they had grown up in.

Sir Dorrian let the children have a quiet

dinner to themselves upstairs in a small sitting room. They did not say much. They were quite tired at this point and had almost run out of things to say. Amy fell asleep before they had finished dinner, and Airdella had to wake her up so that she could put her to bed. When Airdella returned to the sitting area, she found Walter asleep as well. She woke him up and told him they may as well all go to bed. A light rain was falling outside, and the beds were oh so soft. The pitter patter of rain on the roof was just the right touch to lull them off to sleep.

ABOUT THE AUTHOR

Emily G Watson developed a love of story, adventure, and exploration from a young age, living in the deserts of the United Arab Emirates in the Persian Gulf and the rainforests of Singapore in Southeast Asia before her family finally relocated to Sugar Land, Texas. Her adventures both in books and the great big world we call Earth have fueled her imagination and inspired more stories in her head than she could possibly write in one lifetime. She graduated from the University of Houston's Honors College with a BA in History. After teaching US History for six years in a Northwest Houston public high school, Emily decided to make a career change that would allow her the time to purse more goals and interests in life, things which she did not have time for in the busy classroom, high stakes testing, life. She now has a career in the national park service that will afford her more time to explore the outdoors and to pursue her writing.

Her friends know that if they can't find her, she is probably off getting lost in the woods somewhere. She loves fantastic views, warm desert sun, evergreen forests, and the smell of the sea. She seeks to honor Jesus and to pursue His glory wherever it may take her.

Connect with Emily:

thistleboundbooks.wixsite.com/watson

email: thistleboundbooks@yahoo.com

@thistleboundbooks